INTO THE CANYON

INTO THE CANYON

By
Victoria Lourdes Medina Baker

XULON PRESS

Xulon Press
2301 Lucien Way #415
Maitland, FL 32751
407.339.4217
www.xulonpress.com

© 2023 by Victoria Lourdes Medina Baker

Cover Design by: You & I Creative Co.
Photographer: Levi McKay

All rights reserved solely by the author. The author guarantees all contents are original and do not infringe upon the legal rights of any other person or work. No part of this book may be reproduced in any form without the permission of the author.

Due to the changing nature of the Internet, if there are any web addresses, links, or URLs included in this manuscript, these may have been altered and may no longer be accessible. The views and opinions shared in this book belong solely to the author and do not necessarily reflect those of the publisher. The publisher therefore disclaims responsibility for the views or opinions expressed within the work.

Unless otherwise indicated, Scripture quotations taken from the Holy Bible, New International Version (NIV). Copyright © 1973, 1978, 1984, 2011 by Biblica, Inc.™. Used by permission. All rights reserved.

Paperback ISBN-13: 978-1-66286-851-1
Ebook ISBN-13: 978-1-66286-852-8

TABLE OF CONTENTS

```
DEDICATION . . . . . . . . . . . . . . . . . . . . . . . . . . . . . . . . . . . ix
ACKNOWLEDGEMENTS . . . . . . . . . . . . . . . . . . . . . . . . . . xi
INTRODUCTION . . . . . . . . . . . . . . . . . . . . . . . . . . . . . . xiii
```

Chapter 1: "The Valley" 1
Chapter 2: "The New Girl" 7
Chapter 3: "The Fall" 11
Chapter 4: "Getting Closer" 15
Chapter 5: "A Secret" 19
Chapter 6: "Cold Days" 23
Chapter 7: "Carolina" 29
Chapter 8: "Across the Valley" 33
Chapter 9: "An Intense Ride" 37
Chapter 10: "Still Numb" 43
Chapter 11: "More Secrets" 47
Chapter 12: "Back to Normal" 51
Chapter 13: "Thanksgiving Day" 55
Chapter 14: "Winter" 59
Chapter 15: "Christmas Prep" 63
Chapter 16: "Sweet Memories" 69
Chapter 17: "A Clue" 73
Chapter 18: "Handwritings" 77

INTO THE CANYON

Chapter 19: "Grandpa K" 79
Chapter 20: "Bitter Cold" 83
Chapter 21: "A Precious Life" 87
Chapter 22: "Truth Revealed" 89
Chapter 23: "The Talk" 93
Chapter 24: "The Long Ride Home" 97
Chapter 25: "Mid-Winter" 103
Chapter 26: "Spring" 105
Chapter 27: "Anticipation" 107
Chapter 28: "Graduation Day" 113
Chapter 29: "A Man Now" 119
Chapter 30: "Hard Work Pays Off" 123
Chapter 31: "More Lies" 127
Chapter 32: "The Real Truth" 133
Chapter 33: "Life Changes" 137
Chapter 34: "Momma's Turn" 141
Chapter 35: "Making Plans" 147
Chapter 36: "Next Steps" 153
Chapter 37: "Family Meeting" 157
Chapter 38: "MJ" 161
Chapter 39: "Whose Baby is She Anyway?" 167
Chapter 40: "Shower Them with Gifts" 171
Chapter 41: "Endings and Broken Curses" 177
Chapter 42: "The Unending Charade" 181

ABOUT THE AUTHOR 185
FURTHER READING 187

DEDICATION

I dedicate this book to my daddy and all his family, his legacy, as well as the beautiful land where he grew up. He loved us all, and the land with his whole heart.

In 2019 our very loved daddy/paw-paw left this earth. A life of great purpose passed to eternity. He is forever loved and forever missed.

ACKNOWLEDGEMENTS

Thank you to "*You and I Creative Co*." https://www.youand-icreate.co/ Vanessa and Levi McKay, for the front and back cover design. It is breathtaking! The minute I saw the photos, I knew they were meant for this book. They bring the ranch to life. Your talent goes beyond words!

"Thank You" to my children, in birth order:

Jeremy Victor Baker, my first born, who reminds me so much of my daddy and whose heart loves bigger than almost anyone I know. Thank you for being who you are, loving this ranch as much as I do, and for sharing your life and beautiful family with me so freely. You and Eden; Jaycee and Elyn are gems in my heart.

Christopher Joel Baker, the middle child, who shares my middle child syndrome, and my love of creating something beautiful out of simple words. Thank you for sharing ideas in this novel, editing multiple times, writing Paw-Paw's beautiful song, *"The Cowboy,"* your connection to the characters, and enthusiasm to get this book done and printed! You, Paige and Alexis are gems in my heart.

Vanessa Elizabeth (Baker) McKay, whose creativity and amazing ideas surpass anything I could imagine. Thank you for sharing your creativity with me for this book and in life, and for all the editing you did. Your laughter and honesty are inspiring. Thank you to your husband, Levi, for editing and sharing inspiring ideas, not to mention the amazing photography on the front and back of this book! You, Levi, little baby girl and sweet foster children (A, J, E so far) are gems in my heart.

"Thank You" to my husband:

Pastor Vernon Albert Baker, who I could never have gotten through this novel, or this life without. You have taught me what an authentic relationship with Jesus Christ is about. Thank you for encouraging me when I struggled and for challenging me when I felt defeated. You are the diamond in my heart.

INTRODUCTION

In the midst of a beautiful and serene mountain valley is a most unattractive place, not really messy, but simple and drearily plain. A few old cars and pick-ups line up outside, appearing to say, "I'm old, don't try to drive me, I won't take you far, leave me here to die." Yet now and then a creaky engine sound shrieks across the valley, chugging and coughing until the engine warms up and slowly, hesitantly backs down the long dirt drive. The driveway of this home is long and narrow and runs alongside a barbed wire fence, separating property, separating lives, family long ago divided, long ago lost, never to be found again.

CHAPTER 1

"THE VALLEY"

This story began many years before the house existed, many years before the family in the house existed. It began in a time of simplicity, a time of strong family ties. Many families throughout the valley were struggling to survive, just getting by with their ranching and farming. Having each other was enough and they made it work. As things happen in life, there was change and their simple lives became complicated.

The peaceful valley was full of families whose ancestors had come from faraway lands. Most of the families had several generations living together or in compounds so that all were close by each other. They were used to helping each other when times were hard. It was just the way things were supposed to be and it was a happy enough life. The families seemed to get along fine, at least most of them got along.

Izrael was a young and handsome boy. His family had been in the valley for several generations. Izrael loved the valley and the mountains that surrounded it. Many days his mother would look for him and not find him anywhere, but she would always be able to guess where he went. Izrael often disappeared into the canyon of his beloved mountains. He would take off on foot or on his favorite horse, Mindee. She was his from the minute he watched her birth. The moment Mindee and Izrael looked at each other, it was love at first sight. They were inseparable. For the past 11 years the two disappeared together. On the days Izrael chose to head out on foot he ran through the mountain. Running was his escape, from everything. It would start as a walk then faster and faster until finally he found himself running at a very fast pace.

He was known as "Speedy Iz" among his friends. He was the fastest runner at Forrest Lane High School. The nickname had been said so much it had finally stuck. Sometimes even his family called him "Speedy Iz." The days Izrael ran were the days his mother worried about him the most. She wondered what was troubling him and what he was running from, or who.

"Good morning, Momma," Izrael spoke softly as he entered the kitchen which was filled with warm air and wonderful scents permeating down the hallway, to the bedrooms where Izrael's sisters were still sleeping. It was Saturday and that meant the girls could sleep a little later than their usual 5:00 am wake up time during the school week. Izrael was never able to sleep late. He woke up at the same time, day after day, ready and excited to get the day going. Izrael was an energetic soul, always looking for things to keep him busy. "Good morning, son," followed by a glowing smile and a warm hug from his mother. He loved his momma so much. Momma always stood up for Iz, even when he didn't deserve it, and especially when his poppa was angry with him. It never took a lot to make Poppa angry. "I know you're hungry," Momma said playfully, "so grab a plate and fill your belly before you head out to do your chores." "Yes, Momma, thank you, it looks delicious! The best breakfast ever!"

"The Valley"

Suzanah smiled as she watched Izrael dive into his meal. He was always the one to compliment her cooking. Suzanah Grace (Klein) Kammer grew up in the valley, across the wide fields from her husband. She knew him as she grew up and always admired and noticed his handsome features. Even as a little boy Alexander had a strength about him that drew Suzanah to him. He was one of the quiet ones among all the boys she grew up with in the valley. She remembered thinking to herself, when she was about 10 years old, that one day she would marry Alexander Shane Kammer and they would have a beautiful family together. That they did.

Alex K, as he was known in the valley, was a hardworking, strong minded and well-respected rancher. He was well liked by the other ranchers and farmers, always willing to give advice when asked but demanding of his privacy at the same time. Alex K was happy to help a neighbor in need, but he would never let anyone get too close, just Suzanah, his beautiful bride.

Izrael admired both of his parents, even though he felt some fear towards his dad. This fear was centered around great respect for his authority as head of the family. Izrael strived to please him and hoped to be as good of a man as his father one day. His efforts showed daily as he worked very hard on the ranch, always looking for something to do and rarely taking a break, except to eat and visit with Momma.

On this day there was much to be done. Alex K had already started working when Iz showed up in the kitchen. Knowing his dad was at least an hour ahead of him, Iz ate quickly, carried his dishes to the sink, kissed Momma on the cheek and raced to the back door, hardly slowing down enough to grab his jacket and hat. Suzanah watched him hurrying out the door, through the porch, under the big cherry tree and over the hill that led to the vast property Alex K had worked so hard for every day since before they were married.

Iz found his dad working on some fence line far beyond the house. The barbed wire fence had needed mending for a couple of weeks. Alex K was worried some of the cattle might cross over into the neighbors' land which would make it difficult to find them due to the vastness of property everyone in the valley owned. Iz ran all the way from the house to where his dad was working. He stopped just short of where the horses were grazing, just enough to startle his horse, Mindee, who was sleepily grazing in the tall grass. When Mindee let out a neigh of excitement, Alex K looked up and said "Oh, hi Iz, I was expecting you," as if he had seen him coming. Not much startled Poppa, Iz thought to himself. Such a strong and confident man Poppa always was, but Iz also wondered why his dad was so easily angered. This was something Izrael had tried to understand long ago. Maybe he would never really know.

Iz and Alex K worked hard throughout the day, hardly stopping for more than hydration and a quick snack Momma had sent with Alex K earlier in the day. Even as they finished the broken fence line, Poppa was talking about another part of the fence he noticed two days earlier while riding and checking the property lines. This one may have been torn by human hands, but it was hard to tell, other than the fact that there were no signs of animal hair in the barb wire. Regardless, the next several days would, no doubt, include more fence mending.

As soon as they had packed up the tools onto Poppa's horse and small trailer the horse pulled, Iz turned to Mindee who seemed to know it was quitting time. Maybe seeing Iz and his Poppa packing up stirred Mindee into realizing the workday was coming to an end, or maybe the sun setting across the beautiful, quiet valley brought pangs of hunger into her belly. No matter the reason, it was always fun to turn and see Mindee standing tall, as if inviting, or challenging, Iz to jump on her back and ride off into the sunset together. Iz did not disappoint Mindee, running quickly to her and jumping, he threw his right leg over her body and sat boldly, leaning in, to whisper "that-a-girl, let's go!!" Into the canyon the two rapidly rode together. Alex K stood back watching, smiling to himself, and feeling exceptionally good about the land and family he had created. He felt much pride at this moment and would do anything to keep things from ever changing. Anything.

CHAPTER 2

"THE NEW GIRL"

As in every life and every family, things did change through the years as Izrael and his sisters grew older. Life moved on.

The family of 7 were happy, they were healthy, and they had each other. The two older girls, Lucy, and Priscilla kept Suzanah company and helped with chores during the day, since they had graduated two and three years prior. The two younger girls, Josephina, and Nikola, helped after school and on the weekends. Iz worked hard to keep up with his poppa. It was a cool Autumn morning, the day that would begin the slow and steady changes the Kammer family would experience. It was a Monday and classes were about to start, Iz's senior year, the first day of school. All the kids were excited that morning, and Iz could feel the sensation of newness in the crisp morning air as it wafted through the partially opened windows of the classrooms. Izrael had walked his younger sisters to their new classrooms, as they had been nervous that morning, to meet their new teachers.

Josephina was beginning 5th grade and Nikola was just starting 1st grade. Being the youngest in the family, she was well protected by her older siblings with Izrael being the most protective. They arrived early so Iz could be in the classroom with Nikola and make sure she was okay. The minute they walked in, Nikola began talking with a group of girls she knew from church. Izrael smiled, seeing clearly Nikola was fine. He gave her a quick kiss and hug, whispered he loved her and told her to be good. Nikola kissed Iz on the cheek, looked at him with those big blue eyes and said, "I wuv you too, bubba!"

Izrael felt warm and peaceful as he left the younger children's area of the school and began making his way to the high school. Josephina had run off to her friends the minute they hit the school grounds, so he knew she was okay. The high school sat up higher than the elementary school and around a large grouping of trees. It was always a climb but this time of year it was a beautiful climb with the trees' colors changing and the cool fall breeze. Iz thought about what it would be like in a couple of months when it snowed, and he would be trudging through the snow to get to his classroom. He didn't mind. Izrael loved the snow and the outdoors.

As he entered the building and turned to walk towards his classroom, he saw a group of girls talking and giggling among themselves. Iz noticed a new face in the group. Being the curious soul that he was, he stepped closer and heard the new girl say her name was Carolina. The other girls were all whispering and giggling with her when Izrael walked by. He smiled and tipped his hat as he passed. Carolina caught his eye and gave him a spine-tingling wink. Izrael did not know what that meant, and he did not like the way it made him feel so he hurried off to his classroom.

Later that day, as Izrael sat eating his lunch under the big pine tree where he always sat to eat, the new girl, Carolina, approached him, invading his quiet peaceful time. Izrael looked up and noticed she had a rather large head. She wasn't ugly, but neither was she pretty. Her features were dramatic and had a darkness to them, but she had intriguing blue eyes. Her dark hair flowed naturally down her back. She was tall and well rounded, not heavy, but more of what some of his friends referred to the big girls as, "large boned." He realized very quickly that this girl was not shy. She rather loudly said, "So what's your name? Are you shy, or do you talk to girls?" Izrael stood up, looked her almost eye-to-eye and said, "My name is Izrael Shane Kammer, pleased to meet you," as he extended his hand toward Carolina. Carolina accepted his hand, smiled widely and loudly answered, "And my name is Carolina Jane Parker, I am very pleased to meet you, and look at that, our middle names rhyme!" Carolina winked at Izrael again, like she had done in the hallway outside the classroom. Iz looked away quickly and asked if she liked the school. Carolina began quickly talking about the girls she had met and the teacher, and how there are so many boys in the school but the only one she wanted to meet was Izrael. To this Izrael quickly stated, "Oh, did you hear that? It's the first warning bell. I don't want you to be late back to class, on your first day at Forrest Lane!" Speedy Iz turned and hurried off in a different direction back to the building, leaving Carolina alone to make her way back to class.

Izrael managed to avoid further eye contact with the new girl and spent the remainder of his school day with his nose in his books, writing papers and completing his assignments. Iz did not like to take schoolwork home with him in the afternoons because he would much rather find Mindee and go up into the hillside and escape all other realities.

Riding on Mindee, running through the pine trees, sitting on an old tree stump, writing in his journal, and taking in all that the mountain could give him. That was Izrael's world, and he had no desire for anything to interrupt his life. But she already had.

CHAPTER 3

"THE FALL"

By the middle of October, most of the trees had changed colors and the weather had significantly changed from the first day of school in early September. Everyone was in jackets and gloves, expecting the first big snow to hit anytime soon. Alex K had spent the last several weeks stocking up the wood pile and had a few successful hunts and fishing trips, so the ice box was full and ready for the winter. Suzanah, Lucy and Priscilla, had spent most of their time preparing jars of various types of food from jams and jellies to pickles and potatoes. They also stocked the shelves with plenty of homemade bread and prepared spices to use when they cooked the meats Alex K had stored up for the family.

    Izrael and his two younger sisters continued their daily walks to and from school, returning home in the afternoons full of stories and chatter about their day at school. At least Josephina and Nikola had stories, Izrael usually listened to their stories and teased them while they giggled and played. Iz did not talk about school anymore. Suzanah wondered why but she didn't ask. She knew he would tell her when he was ready if there was anything bothering him. She was sure, once he got up from playing with his sisters and headed to the door, he was ready for his escape. Her Speedy Iz would take off running through the property, looking for Mindee and then flying through the pine trees on her back.

Today was no exception. Ignoring the cold air, Speedy Iz ran from the house, up the hillside, all the way to the other side of the hill before he finally found Mindee grazing. Mindee jumped with her front legs punching the air letting out her happy neigh. The two rejoiced in seeing each other as they took off on their usual trails. This time Izrael stopped in one of his favorite spots and pulled out his journal. In an effort to distract himself, Iz sat on a stump and started writing. His words seemed to spill out on the pages without any effort. Izrael always considered himself to be a cowboy and he began to let his soul speak, on old parchment paper:

The cowboy straddles horses, and wears a big sombrero
He shoots it out with outlaws, the Mexican Vaquero

The tough guy rides the ranges, and packs a heavy gun
He sings to horse and cattle, as he rides beneath the sun

Soon the sun was beginning to set. Izrael knew better than to let it get dark. On occasion he would get permission from Momma to take his bed roll and sleep in the canyon, but Momma never liked him to do so in the fall. The weather was too unpredictable in the mountains. Izrael closed his journal and whistled for Mindee who was grazing nearby. She came instantly and they began the ride back home. Iz began talking to Mindee as she galloped out of the canyon, and down the hill. Mindee would grunt and make horse sounds when Iz talked to her, as if she were responding to him. This time he told Mindee about Carolina. It was the first time he had said her name out loud to anyone. Mindee was a safe place to share, always a safe place. The distraction of writing also helped. Izrael knew he could find his soul and clear his mind by writing, especially when he did so in the canyon.

Carolina had been pursuing Izrael since the first day of school. She made it very clear she was interested in being his girlfriend. Izrael had never had a girlfriend and he was very unsure of what that meant, or even how to act around a girl, so he mostly avoided her. Carolina would sit nearby Iz during lunch and talk as loudly as she could. Izrael could not help but hear her stories, all about herself and her momma who had raised her alone. The two had moved into the mountain valley from California over the summer. Carolina said they came to the mountains to seek a peaceful lifestyle and had hopes of being accepted by the families in the valley. Izrael thought to himself, "if you don't talk so loud, maybe people will like you!"

As often occurs in small communities, rumors had begun to spread around the valley that Carolina's mother had stolen money from her own father. Geraldine Parker embarrassed her parents when she became pregnant out of wedlock. Geraldine's parents did not want anyone to know she had a child, so they sent her to distant relatives, until she was run off by those relatives for stealing from them.

Carolina bragged to the girls at school that her grandfather was rich and had given Ms. Parker a lot of money to move to the mountains and start a new life. The girls thought the story missed some truth and added to the rumor–that Ms. Parker had stolen the money.

CHAPTER 4

"GETTING CLOSER"

Carolina and Izrael had nothing in common. In fact, they were so far opposite of each other, it seemed to be what drew them to each other in the first place. Carolina kept Izrael's attention by flirting and teasing him. He liked her long dark flowing hair and those big blue eyes that seemed to dance on their own while she shared her stories. Those same eyes caught Izrael's attention often, and Carolina took every opportunity to catch his attention. She seemed somehow to always be close by. When Izrael walked to class, she would be in the same hallway, when Iz sat down for lunch, Carolina always seemed to be at a table close by, and when school was over for the day, there she was again, standing on the steps outside the front of the school. Izrael found this all both a little annoying, and a little flattering. He had never noticed this kind of attention from a girl before, and he was beginning to like it.

One morning at school, Iz saw Carolina walking towards him carrying a huge pile of books. Iz ran over and offered to carry her books for her. Izrael asked where she was heading. With those big blue eyes, Carolina motioned towards the left, around the long hallway. The two walked towards the classroom where Carolina had been heading. In that walk Izrael began to realize he was developing some feelings for Carolina and he was actually enjoying their conversation.

Each day the two would meet at one end of the long hallway and walk together towards Carolina's class. Each day their conversations became more and more interesting. The two had become somewhat of a couple. Little did either of them know what this would mean for their futures.

As Iz and Carolina got to know each other, Izrael's friends began asking him a lot of questions. They wanted to know what he saw in her, and why he was spending so much time at school with her. Iz found their questions intrusive and soon hardly saw his friends anymore. Almost all of his time was now spent with Carolina.

Even at home, Suzanah was seeing changes in her son, although she did not know it had to do with a girl. One afternoon, soon after Iz and his sisters had arrived home from school and were preparing to start their chores, Izrael opened up to Momma about Carolina. Iz began by telling Momma about the new family of two in the valley and asked if she had heard about them. She nodded quietly, letting Izrael talk freely. Iz went on focusing on Carolina and her ability to capture attention when she wanted it; he talked about her loudness in the lunchroom. He described this was Carolina's way of trying to meet others and make new friends. Momma found it to be an odd way of doing so but kept her thoughts to herself, for she truly wanted Izrael to feel safe sharing his thoughts out loud to her. She had been patiently waiting for several weeks to hear about this and did not want her own opinions to disrupt what he was sharing.

"Getting Closer"

By the time Izrael finished talking, his sisters were hard at work on their afternoon chores and he was far behind on his. He quickly gave Momma a hug and a kiss on the cheek and raced out the door. Iz began looking for Poppa, to help him with the cattle and anything else he might have been working on. Izrael also hoped he would have a little time to journal his thoughts, as his mind had been preoccupied although talking with Momma always helped.

Izrael left Momma feeling a little sad, and a little hopeful for her son. She knew Izrael was a momma's boy, and a loner. These things often worried her about Izrael; all she wanted was for her son to find joy and happiness in his life. Suddenly she heard herself saying out loud, "maybe this girl will be his true love."

CHAPTER 5

"A SECRET"

Suzanah remembered how much Alex K had always worked to keep his own father happy. She could see the similarity now with Izrael, always trying to please his father. It bothered her that Alex K did not see it. He would grumble and complain about Iz, calling him lazy and selfish all the while Izrael was out working the cattle and tending to all the other farm animals that were his responsibility.

Alex K was raised by two very hard working and demanding parents. Frank and Rebekah Kammer had a large family together. Alex K was their oldest. They expected him to carry on the family traditions and there was never room for mistakes. Frank was especially hard on Alex K. If he felt his son was slowing down, he would take him out to the barn, sit him down and talk with him about the seriousness of being the man of the house. Alex K was always respectful, answering his father with "yes sir" type of answers. If anyone asked Alex K now if he had feared his father, he denied it. Suzanah knew better. She remembered the days when Alex K was courting her. Had his parents not liked Suzanah it would have been much harder.

As Suzanah pondered these memories she flashed back to a warm Sunday afternoon, just a few weeks before Suzanah and Alex K were to be married. She and Alex K had gone for a short walk, into the canyon, and were on their way back down the hill when they heard screaming. Alex K stopped dead in his tracks. His face went flush white, he looked deep into Suzanah's eyes and said, "That's Momma screaming! I have to go!!" With that Alex K took off running and was at the bottom of the hill before Suzanah could say anything. In fact, she remembered she was still standing in the same spot when Alex K made it to the house.

When Suzanah caught up with Alex K, she quietly and hesitantly walked into the small house. The front porch was small and opened immediately into the kitchen. Alex K was standing off to the side quietly. Frank stood close to Rebekah but there was another person in the room. Suzanah could see the top of her head. She was wearing a bonnet and her head was turned in the other direction. The room was silent, except for quiet sniffles from Rebekah. Suzanah hurried to Alex K's side and stayed quiet. No one spoke for what seemed like forever.

Finally the woman stood. Suzanah could see that she was not much older than Alex K, and she was quite strong looking, almost manly. She looked straight towards Frank and stated firmly, "I have finished what I came to tell you. Now it is in your court to decide what to do with this information." The young woman walked briskly towards the door and left without another word. Suzanah was afraid to ask what the woman wanted; why she had been there, and why Rebekah had screamed the way she did. The echo of her scream would stay with both Alex K and Suzanah forever. Suzanah chose not to ask. Alex K chose not to talk about it. There was a family

"A Secret"

secret that would remain a secret, for now. The secret was there when Alex K and Suzanah married, and Suzanah still did not know what it was. Inside, she shivered at how it might impact her children's lives. Could it continue into future generations, she wondered to herself? One day she thought, one day she would ask Alex K, but not today. Not today.

CHAPTER 6

"COLD DAYS"

By the time Iz and Alex K had finished up with the outdoor chores and were back at the house, Suzanah and the girls had dinner almost ready. The two went to clean up while the finishing touches were completed. Suzanah had prepared a typical meal for the family which usually included meat, potatoes, vegetables, and homemade bread. Suzanah's dinner rolls were the best in the valley. She often received visitors who would boldly ask if she had any of her rolls prepared and would offer to pay for a dozen or so. Sometimes Suzanah would have enough to spare and other times she would have to admit that her family had eaten them all. Baking bread had become a daily task for Suzanah, and she had grown to love working the dough. Suzanah spent many hours lost in her dough, so to speak. This is when Suzanah could be found singing worship songs or praying aloud, with her eyes open, so she could see the dough. One day Alex K had stopped in at the house during a long day of working to find his wife singing and praying. Suzanah had felt embarrassed but Alex K kept that picture in his mind, as he had told her she had never looked more beautiful than while she was praying and singing to the Lord.

Izrael learned while he was very young that a boy removed his hat when he entered the home, and if someone was praying, he should be very quiet and respect their time. Iz found it peaceful to hear Momma praying, and a feeling of comfort always overwhelmed him deep inside.

Suzanah Grace worked hard to teach her children good manners; she had very strict rules for each of them. Good manners during meals were especially important to Suzanah; she wanted her children to use their napkins appropriately and to ask to be excused before standing up from the table. Suzanah also had another special rule during meals, that was focused solely on Izrael, especially once he became a teenager. Iz knew he had a bad habit of staring at his sisters' plates as the meal would begin to wind down. He would sit, looking like a vulture ready to pounce on his prey, that is until Suzanah gave him that look which silently told him, he better stop staring! It took Suzanah a long time to get Izrael to learn not to stare at the girls' plates, but rather to wait patiently. If any of them could not finish he would be expected to wait until their leftovers were offered to him. Izrael was required to respond with, "Yes, please" as he calmly accepted the leftovers. This was a test of patience for Izrael, a test he sometimes failed, and failing only made it worse because Suzanah would make Izrael take all the leftovers out to the pig troughs rather than getting to enjoy them himself.

Izrael noticed that dinner tonight looked especially delicious and was a little worried there might not be leftovers on his sisters' plates. Maybe Iz had worked harder and had a bigger appetite tonight, but he thanked Momma more than usual which always made her smile, but also made her a little suspicious. Being the only boy out of five children, Speedy Iz had the biggest appetite. Momma gently reminded Iz, "remember your manners, Son," and winked quickly with a slight grin on her face. Iz was beginning to feel impatient nearing the end of the meal but tried to not look anxious as he waited to see if any of his sisters left anything on their plates. Finally, they were finished and Iz had his full share of their leftovers. He had succeeded this time and he was so relieved. It was truly a very delicious meal, "the best meal ever, Momma!" Izrael said as he wiped his mouth after his last bite and quickly carried his dish to the sink where Lucy and Priscilla had already begun washing. Priscilla gave Lucy a quick roll of her eyes as they both giggled with Momma who always enjoyed these kinds of moments with her children.

Once the kitchen was cleaned up, Izrael and his sisters began the process of taking turns in the bathroom. A family of 7 with two bathrooms could make for a long night. They had worked out a good routine, so most nights went fairly smoothly. Iz was usually the last one to get in the bathroom, being the only brother with 4 sisters. Often there was not enough hot water for him so he would clean himself up really fast and jump into bed to warm up.

It was a cold night and the fire in the wood burning stove had dwindled low. Izrael covered himself up and slowly drifted into a deep sleep, dreaming of hills and Mindee and riding for hours. These were Izrael's typical dreams every night. Tonight, he woke up with a start in the middle of the night. He had dreamed that Carolina was riding on Mindee and Mindee was not cooperating. Mindee kept throwing her head back and making sounds that Izrael recognized as not very nice. No matter what Iz tried to do, he could not stop Mindee from trying to throw Carolina off her back. When Izrael woke up he was sweating. He had been trying to yell at Mindee to stop but his voice would not yell. He realized it was a bad dream and crawled back under the covers. What was that about, he wondered? "Why would I dream that Mindee did not like Carolina?" His thoughts slowly softened as he gradually fell back to sleep.

The next morning came too soon, and way too cold. The girls and Izrael began the morning routine mixed with bathroom turns, eating what Momma had prepared for their breakfast, and their morning chores. It was somewhat of an orchestrated routine. Each child knew when it was their turn for the next step. They seemed to move in a rhythm; again, this family of 7 moving swiftly through their turn for each part. Izrael had a lot on his mind this particular cold morning. His dream about Mindee and Carolina was still bothering him. Iz wished he could take time to journal. Part of him wished it was not a school day, and the other part was looking forward to a day of classwork to keep his mind occupied. Izrael always left early with his younger sisters, as their walk to school was just shy of 2 miles. He continued the routine of walking Josephina and Nikola to their perspective rooms. Once they were safe in their classrooms he would hurry off to the hallway where he met Carolina every school morning.

Today, she was nowhere to be seen. Izrael waited and waited. The first bell rang and still no Carolina. The second bell rang, and he knew better than to let any more time go by before getting to his own classroom. Izrael had learned the hard way his freshman year. He and his buddies were outside one day after lunch, talking and laughing so hard they didn't hear the first bell. By the time the second bell rang they were already late for class. When they got to the front of the building, the principal, Mr. Fischer, was standing holding a stick in one hand and tapping his other hand with the same stick. He was not happy. One by one, as the boys scurried up the steps, Mr. Fischer gave each boy a paddle. Each boy answered with, "Thank you, Mr. Fischer, and I am sorry I am late." This was the ritual that every child at Forrest Lane High School endured if they were late to class. It may not have seemed like a very harsh punishment to some people, but Izrael was humiliated to receive a paddle from the principal. He never wanted to see Momma's face look so disappointed like she had the day he was paddled last year, after reading the principal's note Iz took home.

The day went on, classroom time seemed to last forever. Izrael was anxious to look for Carolina during lunch period. That too came and went, and still no Carolina. He wondered to himself what could have happened to keep her from being at school. It was not like her to miss. Carolina, as tough and hard as she appeared on the outside, loved to learn. Her favorite class was writing which surprised Iz. She had told him that writing was her own creative outlet. She could write all her feelings down and then forget about them. This was something Izrael had never learned how to do, as his writing seemed to continue in his mind, as if it would never stop. Iz also loved math and science. He enjoyed making numbers do things and he was fascinated by the way the two subjects worked together.

The last bell of the day had rung. Izrael began his trek to the elementary school building to pick up his little sisters. Nikola was already racing towards him with a big smile on her face and yelling out, "Bubba, Bubba, I'm here, I'm here!" Iz ran towards her and scooped her up, spinning her around until she squealed with delight. "Come on," Iz told Nikola, "Let's go get Phina," as the family often referred to Josephina, "she will be ready when we get to her classroom!" Josephina was standing outside the building when Iz and Nikola skipped around the corner and saw her. "Phina, Phina!" Nikola rang out and the three continued their skipping to the end of the school property. The walk home always seemed longer than the walk to school in the morning, and today was no exception.

CHAPTER 7

"CAROLINA"

It was the end of another week. School kept everyone busy with classwork and sports. Izrael loved sports. His favorite was basketball. He was fast, or "speedy," on the court. During practice on this particular Friday Iz was distracted. Carolina had not been to school all week. It wasn't like her to not be there. He wondered if she was sick. Iz decided, as he dribbled the ball up and down the court, he would go to her house over the weekend to find out why she had missed school.

Suddenly Iz heard, "Heads up, Speedy Iz!" There was a basketball flying towards him. Iz spun around, dropped the ball he had been dribbling and caught the incoming ball. Speedy Iz took off towards the basketball goal, flew by his teammate, Benji, who was trying to defend him, and swished it! He could hear whooping and hollering behind him. Iz loved when he did things like this. He realized he had been distracted and not really paying attention to basketball practice. His friends noticed too. Afterwards, as the guys were cleaning up in the locker room, his best friend, Marcus Joe, or MJ as everyone knew him best, pulled Izrael aside and asked what was going on. MJ put his hand on Izrael's shoulder as he faced him, indicating he was concerned for his friend. Izrael looked up at MJ who was about 8 inches or so taller than Iz and smiled. "Thanks for asking, MJ, I'm just a little distracted. Carolina hasn't been at school all week." "Oh, girls!" MJ exclaimed! "Come on, I'll race you across the court," and off the two raced with Speedy Iz naturally getting there first. MJ had done a good job of getting Izrael through his distraction but not completely from his mind.

Friday nights were Izrael and his sisters' favorite nights of the week. "Family Night," as Momma and Poppa referred to Friday evenings was full of a light dinner followed by playing board games, snacking on popcorn, and drinking hot cocoa. If it was someone's birthday they also had cupcakes. Izrael loved Friday nights. It was the one time everyone seemed happy, even Poppa relaxed and laughed with the family, although sometimes he was too quiet.

The family settled in with their snacks and started pulling out games. With such a big family there was often more than one game going at the same time. Izrael's older sisters, Lucy and Priscilla, or "Cilla" as the family often called Priscilla always wanted to play cards. They loved winning and tonight was no exception. Lucy would always start out saying something like, "Because I am the oldest, I will go first" as she shuffled the deck and passed out the cards as fast as she could. There was always a little bit of competition between Lucy and Cilla, with Lucy being the pushier of the two. Cilla would often shrink back and let Lucy take over just to avoid the fit Lucy might throw if Cilla was too forceful. Tonight, everyone seemed happy. There was so much laughter in the room, the louder the family got, Momma declared she thought their voices would carry into the canyon through the neighbors' front door! This only made the family laugh more and even louder. It was a special night, one they would not forget, as the joy was soon to change within the Kammer family. One day too soon.

CHAPTER 8

"ACROSS THE VALLEY"

Saturday morning began as usual. Early breakfast, morning chores and family chatter. Izrael, Momma noticed as soon as he came to the breakfast table, was distracted and more quiet than usual. She knew better than to start his day with questions so she left him alone in his quietness, knowing he would talk if he wanted to, and when he wanted to. Momma's biscuits and gravy did help Iz get through the morning. He felt somewhat renewed and encouraged by the comfort food that only Momma could provide. He had eaten meals his older sisters cooked when Momma was under the weather, but nothing tasted as delicious or fulfilling as his Momma's cooking. Izrael felt a closeness to Momma that he had not had with anyone else, until Carolina came into his life. But even that was different. He could never share with Carolina the way he shared with Momma.

The morning seemed to drag by forever, as Iz began to feel anxious about asking Poppa if he could take Mindee and ride out across the valley to where Carolina and her mother lived. Poppa was never happy when one of his children wanted to leave the property for anything other than school or errands, he might send them on. Poppa was not as agitated as he often was during the morning chores, so Iz thought it might be a good time to talk with Poppa about Carolina. Izrael started out, "Poppa, can I talk with you about something, ... or someone?" Poppa looked up from rope he was rolling up to pack into the back of his old pickup. He looked surprised but answered, "Yes, son, you can always talk with me about anything," going back to the rope. Izrael took a deep breath and began to tell Poppa about Carolina. Poppa listened closely, looking up into Izrael's eyes occasionally but mostly looking at his rope as he rolled it in slowly. When Izrael stopped talking their eyes met. The silence seemed to last forever until Poppa finally asked, "Are you falling for this girl, Iz?" Izrael paused a few seconds and said, "I don't know, Poppa. I do know that I care about what happens to her, and she was out of school all last week. No one seemed to know why. That is why I am asking your permission, sir, to take Mindee and ride out across the valley to where she and her mother, Miss Geraldine Parker live." Poppa paused again; this time Izrael began to wonder if he would ever speak again. Finally, Poppa stood, set the rope down, walked over in front of Izrael, looked him straight in the eyes and said, "Grandpa K had a way of knowing the difference between a good girl and a not-so-good girl, Iz, and I want you to be very careful about this girl, son. You need to learn how to know the difference in girls. This one may be trouble. For some reason, I don't have a good feeling." Izrael opened his mouth to speak but Poppa put his hand up and continued, "I do trust you and your judgment, Izrael, so if you want to go check on this girl and her mother, go ahead. I want you home before supper, do you understand that?" Izrael nodded quickly. Poppa then continued sternly, "Do not let yourself get alone with this girl at any time. Make sure you have a friend, her mother, one of your sisters, or anyone with you when you are with Carolina. Can you promise me that, Izrael?"

"Yes, sir," Izrael promised Poppa he would follow his advice and hurriedly began packing up tools and everything that went back into the old pickup. The two spent the remainder of their time together in silence. The silence made Izrael uncomfortable, but he shrugged it off and began to focus on what he would do when they finished the chores.

Lunch was ready when Poppa and Izrael arrived back to the house. Momma, Lucy, and Priscilla had everything out on the table. The younger girls were playing in their room when Momma called out, "Lunch!" so that everyone would sit together to eat. After a quick prayer by Izrael, he ate fast and asked to be excused to get Mindee ready. Poppa nodded and after taking his plate and utensils to the kitchen sink Izrael said goodbye and raced out the door, avoiding eye contact with Momma. "There goes Speedy Iz!" Nikola blurted out and everyone laughed, except Momma. She kept her gaze on Poppa as if to say, "What are you not telling me?" who motioned he would tell her later. Momma nodded and went back to her own meal.

Mindee was waiting anxiously, as she always seemed to be, when Izrael raced into the corral to her side. She whinnied loudly and Iz gave her a quick squeeze of her head and rubbed the front of her face. Mindee seemed to know they were going somewhere and Izrael was in a hurry to get away, before Poppa changed his mind.

CHAPTER 9

"AN INTENSE RIDE"

The only sound Izrael could hear was the beating of his own heart, even with the loud clopping sound Mindee made when she trotted. Izrael was nervous, nervous for what he would find when he arrived at Carolina's home, nervous for what she, or her mom, would say to him, and nervous for what he might say to them.

Thoughts raced through his mind over the 40-minute ride which seemed to take longer, in Izrael's mind. He had never been out to visit Carolina at her home. He had met her in an orchard a mile, or so, from her house once. Izrael remembered that day well. Carolina had begged him to meet her there one day after school. Izrael was hesitant because she would not tell him why she wanted to meet. Because he was nervous about being alone in the orchard with Carolina, Izrael had taken his best buddy, MJ, along. The two friends rode horseback to the orchard, laughing loudly along the way, about anything and everything. Carolina told him she could hear them coming from "5 miles away!" He doubted that but laughed when she said it because MJ had the funniest look on his face as she blurted it out to them. Carolina had been upset with Izrael for taking MJ along to meet her in the orchard. He never asked her why she was angry, but he had a feeling she did not like MJ very much. She seemed to have a snarl on her face when she looked at him, but always changed quickly to sort of a fake smile by the time MJ would make eye contact with Carolina. The two never seemed to like each other.

Izrael's thoughts quickly came back to what he was doing when Mindee slowed her pace and began to make snorting sounds. She always did so when she was uneasy. Izrael felt uneasy himself as they approached a very large, old truck parked to the side of the road. The truck engine was on and had a loud almost coughing sound, like it needed to clear its' throat. Izrael and Mindee approached the truck slowly and quietly. The driver appeared to be sleeping. His head was hanging over to one side and his mouth was wide open. That may have been what Izrael heard as they approached. Mindee made a loud snort and the driver jumped, wiped his mouth, and sat straight up, as if he had just gotten into trouble. Izrael smiled, tipped his hat and said, "Hello, sir, I didn't mean to disturb you." The driver, still unsure of his surroundings, cleared his throat and loudly responded, "Oh, you ain't bothering me, son! I was just, uh, just resting my eyes before the long road ahead of us." "Us?" Izrael echoed. "Yes, me and those two crazy females back that-a-away," as he pointed behind the truck and up towards the short hillside in front of Izrael.

Izrael's heart raced, "two females?" he wondered out loud, could it be Carolina and her mother the driver was referring to? Izrael politely thanked the driver, tipped his hat again and pulled back on Mindee's reigns signaling her to take off quickly. They raced around the corner at the top of the hill and as they reached the top, Izrael could see the rooftop of a home. It was sort of an ugly green with dark brown trim around the windows and front door. They were close enough to see that the trim needed some fresh paint.

Izrael had slowed Mindee down again and rubbed her neck to keep her quiet as they approached the house. Once in front of the house, Izrael jumped off Mindee and hung her reigns over a nearby post that almost seemed to be waiting for them. Izrael took a quick glance at Mindee, gulped and walked towards the front steps. The steps were steep and narrow. The house appeared to need much repair. Izrael was one step shy of reaching the top when the door flung open and a large woman holding a small rifle made him jump and fall backwards, nearly falling all the way back down the stairs. "Who are you and what do you want?" the woman screeched at Izrael. Iz could hardly catch his breath when the woman stomped down to the steps below him. Izrael didn't see her go by him; it was almost as if she flew over the top of his head. He spun around quickly, stood up straight, took off his hat and answered, "Hello, ma'am, my name is Izrael Shane Kammer, and I am here to …." The woman interrupted Iz mid-sentence and loudly said, "You better not be looking for Carolina! She ain't here and she sure wouldn't want to see you!"

Izrael found himself very confused. He rubbed the top of his head before putting his hat back on then looked the woman straight into her eyes and said, "Ms. Parker, I am sorry if I frightened you. I am a friend of Carolina's, and I was worried about her because she hasn't been to school all week. I simply wanted to see if she was okay." Geraldine Parker looked Izrael up and down, as if to be deciding how much he was worth. She stepped from one side of him to the other, never letting go of her small rifle. Finally, Izrael asked Ms. Parker if she would put down the rifle. Ms. Parker quickly responded, "when I'm ready to put my rifle down, I'll put it down!" The two stood in silence for what seemed like forever when finally Ms. Parker began walking towards the porch. She glanced towards Izrael and invited him to have a seat on the porch.

Izrael followed Carolina's mother up the steps, feeling very uncertain of what was to come. He never expected to have the experience he was having.

As the two approached some empty chairs to the right of the front door, the door flung open again, this time it was Carolina. Izrael stared at her in amazement and finally blurted out, "So, you ARE here, Carolina!" "What? Yes, of course I'm here, I live here," Carolina answered quickly while looking over at her mother. "Where else would I be?" she added. Izrael started to walk towards Carolina when Ms. Parker stepped in between them. "There'll be none of that!" she said even louder than the last time she spoke. "Momma!" Carolina screeched, "What is wrong with you?"

"What is wrong with ME?" Ms. Parker yelled at full volume this time. Izrael wanted to run. He looked down at Mindee who seemed to be watching the whole episode. "This boy shows up at my house looking for you and he doesn't have the decency to apologize to me!" Izrael gasped, "Apologize, ma'am? What am I to apologize for?" "Just look at her! Can't you see she's pregnant?!" Izrael turned towards Carolina and his mouth dropped, "P-p-p-pregnant? Really?"

Carolina was furious with her mother for blurting out this news. She wanted to be the one to explain to Izrael what had happened. She began to cry, and screech again. Izrael didn't know what to say, or what to do next. He just stood on the porch, wishing he had never gone looking for Carolina in the first place. Several minutes went by and the three stood on the porch in silence. Finally, Ms. Parker set the rifle down on a bench and sat down next to it. She took a deep breath and with an almost crying sound in her voice, asked Izrael frankly, "So, what are you going to do about this?"

Izrael was stunned. He didn't know what to say. What was Ms. Parker asking him? Better yet why was she asking him what he was going to do? Izrael was upset with Carolina too. He was angry because she had not told him she was expecting a child. He had noticed she was a little plump around the middle but never thought there was a baby growing inside her! Izrael had never been with a girl in that way and preferred not to know too much about how these things happen. His racing thoughts were again interrupted by Ms. Parker loudly repeating herself, "What are you going to do about this?" This time Izrael answered quickly and said, "Why are you asking me that? I had nothing to do with this, ma'am!"

Ms. Parker got up, walked over to Carolina who had quietly moved to an empty chair on the porch, and said, "I thought you told me the boy's name was Izrael!" Izrael couldn't believe what he was hearing. No, he thought, that is impossible! By now Carolina was crying. The tears were flowing heavily down her face, her eyes puffed up almost instantly and she yelled out to Izrael, "Tell her the truth, you made me have sex with you! I didn't want to, but you kept pushing until we finally did it. Don't lie, Izrael Shane Kammer, don't you dare lie!"

Izrael didn't know what to do, or what to say. He had never touched Carolina in any way and certainly had not had sex with her! But here he was, standing on this beat up old porch, being accused of getting Carolina pregnant. What was he going to do? In that moment all he wanted to do was run. So he did.

INTO THE CANYON

He ran off the porch, down to Mindee, quickly hopped onto her back and raced off the property as quickly as he could. By this time, Izrael was sweating and crying, and yelling at the top of his lungs, "I DIDN'T DO THIS!!!" What Izrael did not realize that day was that this was only the beginning, the beginning of the lies.

CHAPTER 10

"STILL NUMB"

When Izrael arrived home, it was almost dusk. Dusk was a busy time on a ranch and today was no exception. Alex K had been keeping an eye out for Izrael for the last 45 minutes, or so, and took a deep sigh of relief when he heard the sound of Mindee clopping up the road, near the house. Alex K had just started the evening rounds, checking the cattle and each corner of the rugged property his father had passed down to him. Alex K was very proud of the family property and had high hopes of passing the land down to his own son. That's the way families handled property, the respectable families, he thought to himself. Alex K had worried about Izrael that afternoon, not having a good feeling about the family the girl Izrael was courting came from. He just did not realize, at that moment, how accurate his feeling was.

Izrael hurried near the corral still sitting on Mindee's back. He guided her close to the watering trough so she could refresh herself which she did instantly. Iz slid off her back and wiped his still damp face with his shirt tail which he then quickly tucked into his pants. Poppa was insistent Izrael keep his appearance neat even when working. He would tell

Izrael that a neat appearance gave the impression of an honest, and hardworking, man. Iz always wanted to please Poppa and make him proud so he never argued this with Poppa.

As Iz waited for Mindee to get enough water, his mind wandered back to his ride coming home. He had left Carolina's house abruptly and wondered to himself if the man sitting in the old truck, just below the Parker's home, noticed him racing by, or if Izrael had been a blur. That's what the ride home felt like now to Iz. It felt like a dark, scary blur. Izrael shook his head and almost neighed like Mindee but jumped when she nuzzled under his elbow that she was ready. Izrael jumped back on Mindee and the two shot off, up the hill, into the safety of the beautiful canyon in front of them.

Izrael always felt safe in the canyon. He claimed the canyon as his own, even though it truly belonged to the entire family with Poppa as the head of the family being the owner. Iz dreamed often of the day it would all be his.

His thoughts quickly returned to reality when he saw Poppa ahead of him, on his own horse, rather than in his pickup truck which was what Poppa usually did. Izrael wondered out loud, "Why is Poppa on his horse?" Poppa heard him and turned towards Iz and yelled out, "There you are! I was wondering if you were coming back!" As Izrael approached, Poppa continued, "Did you take care of what you went out there to do, son?" "Uh-hu, …. Sir! Yes, Sir," was Izrael's only response and the two went on to the task at hand, working the cattle and getting them back together for the night.

When they had finished Izrael walked quickly towards Mindee. Poppa was already on his horse. "Let's take a long ride home, over the top of this mountain, Iz." "Yes, Sir," Izrael answered, and the long silent ride began. By the time they arrived home, Izrael realized he was starving, and he strangely felt better. He and Poppa had not said a word to each other but there was a strange sort of comfort, just riding side by side up and over the majestic mountain which lined their property. Izrael, for a few moments, felt as if time stood still and everything that happened earlier seemed to have vanished, but only for a short while. The worst was yet to come.

CHAPTER 11

"MORE SECRETS"

Weekends never lasted long enough, even with extra chores that were required during the weekend, Izrael preferred chores versus being in school. He loved hard manual labor. It kept him strong and useful. Without strength and mobility, he thought to himself, where would he be? It was a cold morning, and the three Kammer children began their walk to school. The wind was blowing just enough to make it feel colder than it really was. Izrael had to coax Nikola along a few times, to get her to walk faster. All she wanted was to snuggle into Izrael's side to stay warm, but it slowed them down too much. Izrael distracted his sisters with stories during their walks. He often told them what it looked like on the other side of their mountain and would make up stories about monsters or ghosts who lived on that other side. This morning he talked about the monsters and kept Nikola so distracted she was surprised how fast they arrived at school!

After their usual arrival routine at the school, Izrael found himself staring down the hallway, as if to expect to see Carolina hurrying up the hall towards him, smiling the way she did. He quickly turned and headed towards his own classroom, determined to keep himself occupied to avoid thinking about what happened when he went to see Carolina over the weekend.

Classes came and went and suddenly it was time for lunch. Izrael wondered what he used to do for lunch, before Carolina had shown up in the valley, had appeared at Forrest Lane High, and in his life. He started looking for his buddies. The four of them had been inseparable, before Carolina; Iz shook his head to keep his thoughts clear. The Four Musketeers, everyone called them. MJ, Benji, Cliff and Iz had been friends since kindergarten, and even a little before that when their mothers would visit each other but their friendships began in kindergarten. They told each other everything, until the last few months, things were different now. So very different.

Izrael headed towards the far end of the lunchroom with his lunch tray, looking for his friends. Finally, he found them, right where they had always eaten together. When Iz walked up the three had been huddled down whispering. Izrael broke up the whispers with a solid, "Hi guys! What's new?" Benji jumped so high he nearly knocked Cliff off the bench they were sharing. MJ stood up and made room for Izrael to join them. "What's going on, guys? Why so serious?" Cliff and Benji stared at MJ as if waiting for him to do all the talking. MJ didn't hesitate, and started asking Iz questions, one after another. Why was he alone, what happened to Carolina, what was going on, and was he okay? Izrael held up his hands, "Woah, MJ, what's with all the questions? I don't know, she just isn't here, okay?!" "You don't know where she is, do you, Speedy Iz? MJ queried, "well, do you?" "No! Not really, I mean, no, I don't know," Izrael said quickly looking down at his lunch suddenly not feeling very hungry. It was the truth. Carolina and Ms. Parker had everything packed and a moving truck ready. Izrael had no idea where they were going, or what their plans were. He felt sad, but didn't want his buddies to know that so he quickly added, "Why would I care anyway?"

The guys all looked at each other and then at Iz, but no one said anything else. The Four Musketeers were back together, sitting at their table they had shared for the last several years. Finally, Izrael was back with them. No one wanted to mess that up. The secrets continued and Iz knew where he could store them to keep them safe. He looked forward to the evening at home, safe in his room where he would journal all his thoughts and fears about Carolina.

Chapter 12

"Back to Normal"

Life seemed to fall back into a normal pattern for Iz, with Carolina and Ms. Parker out of the valley. He sometimes thought about Carolina and her incessant talking and laughing. He did like how she laughed; it seemed to come from deep inside her and echo through the halls at school or the valley when they were all outside. Izrael's friends always seemed annoyed with how she laughed because they would roll their eyes and cover their ears every time she laughed loudly.

It was almost Thanksgiving. The season of fall, which was Izrael's favorite, always went by too fast. The cold, crisp air was almost intolerable during the long walks to school. Izrael and his little sisters would get very excited when Poppa offered to drive them on snowy days. On those days they could hardly see the road in front of them. Poppa would pat Nikola's knee to console her when she screamed if the truck slid on ice. Izrael and Phina thought it was fun and would squeal with delight. Getting a ride to school in Poppa's truck was a special treat, as it did not happen very often.

On this particular morning Poppa had other places to go after dropping the 3 off at school so he was in a hurry, and he wasn't very happy that he had to wait for Phina to finish tying her hair up. Phina was so particular about how her hair looked. When she finally dashed out the front door, Poppa had nearly left her behind. Momma popped her head out the door long enough to remind Poppa to pick up the turkey for Thanksgiving, on his way back home. Poppa tipped his cap towards Momma and winked. As little as the two seemed to talk to each other, Izrael could see how much they loved each other. He wondered, to himself, if he would ever find that kind of love in his life. He hoped so, but he knew who she would never be!

The excitement of the coming Holiday was in the air at school too. In class the teachers had the children doing everything from making paper turkeys to writing essays about their favorite Thanksgiving memory. It felt good to be at school, Izrael thought to himself, and he was finding peace with his uneasiness about what had happened with Carolina. Izrael focused on how much he loved to write. It helped him relax and he especially loved writing poems. His teachers always complimented Iz on his poems. It was becoming a special gift. In the midst of the Thanksgiving fun Izrael sat down to write a poem about his family.

It's Thanksgiving week and my mind is so full
How can I write a poem when my thoughts ….

It wasn't coming to him. This poem wasn't making sense and Izrael knew why. Thoughts of Carolina and the last time he saw her kept interrupting his mind. The screaming, the crying, the accusations. Iz shook his head. One thing he was thankful for was that Carolina and her mother had left the valley. He tried hard to comfort himself with these thoughts, but he could not shake the feeling that they would be back. He hoped not, but he still worried.

    Izrael felt gratitude when the end of the day school bell rang. Speedy Iz hurried outside and then ran towards the building where his sisters were waiting. Izrael's friends were trying to catch up with Iz but they never could catch him. When they did finally catch up outside of Nikola's classroom, MJ stepped in front of Iz to ask him if he was okay. "I'm doing great, MJ, why do you keep asking me that? Come on, let's head home, it is really cold out here!"

    As the Kammer children arrived home they all cheered when they entered the house. The aroma of baking bread and pies had filled the house and all 3 yelled out together, "Three cheers for Momma! Hip, Hip, Hooray!" Momma laughed out loud and hugged the girls as they dropped their wet jackets and slipped off their boots. Izrael kissed Momma on the cheek and hugged her quickly. Thank you for making the house smell so good, Momma," he said happily. He could hardly wait to taste it all! "Tomorrow, Izrael, tomorrow! Tomorrow is Thanksgiving, and we indeed have so much to be thankful for," Momma declared with a big smile on her face. Izrael smiled back at Momma. She looked so very happy. He never wanted that to change.

CHAPTER 13

"THANKSGIVING DAY"

Thanksgiving Day, in the Kammer family, started early. The turkey had to be dressed and prepared to cook for hours. Izrael never understood why a turkey took so much longer to cook than any other food Momma ever made for the family. This thought made him even more impatient about waiting for the big meal. When Iz walked into the kitchen, all 4 sisters and Momma were working away. Momma turned to greet Izrael and gestured towards the table for his breakfast. Momma always made "holiday biscuits" as the family had started calling them one year when Momma had gotten up even earlier than usual to make sure the family had fresh biscuits. There was always a fresh batch of Momma's jam to spread on top and a fresh cup of hot tea or cocoa. Izrael happily prepared and ate 4 biscuits before Momma could tell him he had eaten enough. He jumped up from the table and asked to be excused to go out and check Mindee. Momma just smiled in response.

It was a very cold morning, so Iz wore multiple layers before heading out the door. He was thankful it was not windy, as no number of layers would prevent those winter winds from getting all the way down to his bones. Izrael pulled his wool cap down to cover his ears and stepped off the porch. As he began walking, he could hear the outside sounds. He loved the way the mountains sang in the morning. It was as if every critter sang a morning greeting all at the same time. He found himself stepping in tune with the singing. No words were sung, only the melodious sounds of animal life filled the cold air. There was absolutely no other place Izrael ever wanted to be but on the Kammer family ranch. His whole life he always knew he would never leave the ranch. He wanted to stay and work with Poppa forever.

Poppa was watching Izrael as he walked towards where he was standing. Poppa had stepped out of the house shortly before Iz, so he was not far away. He had just begun walking through the circle of pens where the smaller animals were kept. "Come on over and help me, Izrael, don't be lazy!" Speedy Iz knew he better get there quickly, or Poppa would get angry and continue calling him lazy. He tried so hard not to give that impression. It was as if Poppa wanted him to be lazy! When Iz approached the pigs were eating and chomping loudly on their breakfast. He and Poppa stayed by the fence and watched for a few minutes before either one spoke.

Poppa started, "Have you gotten over that girl crush, Iz?" Izrael did not expect that question at that moment but quickly answered, "She and her momma moved away, Poppa. They are not in the Valley anymore." "That's not what I asked you, Izrael. Have you gotten over that crush you had on her? Girls are trouble and I need your focus to be on your schoolwork and your work on the ranch." "Oh, yes, Sir, I am over her. I am keeping up with my schoolwork and I love working on the ranch with you, Poppa. That will never change." Poppa didn't say another word; but he did give Izrael a look that seemed to say, "I hope not." It wasn't Poppa's usual stern expression. It made Izrael sad to see Poppa look at him that way. He felt like Poppa was disappointed in him for something, only he did not know what it was. He never knew because Poppa would never tell him.

The rest of the day was filled with Thanksgiving festivities which basically meant that everyone ate a lot and enjoyed each other's company. It was just the 7 of them; Izrael, his 4 sisters and their parents. Life was simple, and it was good. They joked and laughed and finished the day off with a family game night. Oh, yes, life was very good.

CHAPTER 14

"WINTER"

Like all holiday weekends, this one went by too quickly. Before they knew it, it was Monday morning again and the cold walk to school was upon the Kammer children, and all the school children in the valley. As they walked, the 3 talked about what they wanted for Christmas. Gifts were small and simple, but it was always fun to open them.

As the school day began, Izrael thought of Carolina and realized he had not thought about her all weekend, only when Poppa asked if he had gotten over her. He was a bit relieved to realize that things were getting back to how they should be before he had met Carolina.

The 4 Musketeers palled around in the school courtyard until the bell rang. It was time to get back to work in the classroom. Izrael worked hard at school too. He loved learning and was always eager to learn something new. Because he was so good at math, many of his friends would ask Iz for help when they didn't understand something in math. The teachers were helpful, but they were often helping other students so Izrael became somewhat of a tutor in math, especially for some of the younger students. One of Izrael's favorite teachers was his high school math teacher, Mr. Bacon. Often Mr. Bacon would tell Izrael he should become a math teacher, because of how easy it was for him and how well he explained it to the other students. Izrael would politely thank Mr. Bacon for the compliment and then talk about how helpful math skills are for running a ranch, and how Poppa had to use math to estimate purchases for feed and so many other parts of the ranch. Mr. Bacon would say, "I know, Iz, you have your plans, and I am sure you will use your math skills well in whatever you do." Mr. Bacon was such an encourager for Iz; he had helped him in many ways throughout his high school years. He would miss him after graduation.

"Graduation?" Izrael spoke out loud, the minute the word popped in his head. His buddy, MJ, was sitting behind him and said, "Shhh, Iz, we aren't supposed to talk during class!" Izrael apologized and went back to reading the textbook, which was not very interesting. Again, Iz put all his efforts into everything he did so he turned his attention back to the book.

As the next few weeks went by, the school began to transform into a winter wonderland. One of Izrael's favorite Christmas songs was, *"I'm Dreaming of a White Christmas,"* and this year was beautiful. There was so much snow on the ground that most of the students who walked to and from school had made themselves snowshoes to keep from sinking into the snow drifts. Izrael had made some for himself and his two little sisters. The girls were so excited to try them out but soon discovered it would take some practice to get used to walking in them. The three would see who could take the biggest steps in the snow and laugh when one of them tumbled and covered himself, or herself in snow! They would sing and talk and laugh all the way, and were usually wet and cold when they arrived, whether at school or at home. Arriving home wet was never an issue. Momma was the best momma in the valley. She always had warm socks for her children to change into and had hot cocoa waiting on the stove. Christmas was such a very special time in the valley, and in the Kammer home.

CHAPTER 15

"CHRISTMAS PREP"

The long-awaited Christmas break from school had finally come. Everyone in the family was excited to spend time together, except Poppa. He would grumble and talk about chores and lazy kids until Momma would give him a look and he would quiet down. It was always enough to keep everyone on their toes trying not to make Poppa mad.

Each day was filled with work, whether inside the Kammer house, or outside tending to the animals and land. Even with so much work to do, there was still time for tree trimming and decorating, and baking, and Christmas story reading going on in the house. Before any of this could take place, the big family outing to go out and find the perfect tree had to come first. This was a Kammer family tradition that went back several generations of Kammer families, on the Kammer ranch. For this outing, all the girls would join, even Momma bundled up and put on her warm hiking boots in search of the perfect tree.

The younger girls would usually get everyone singing, "*Jingle Bells*" the minute they started out, until the older girls could take it no longer and would ask Poppa to tell them the stories of how the Christmas tree hunting started on the ranch so many years ago. Poppa loved telling the stories and everyone loved listening as they trudged through the deep snow, one step at a time, into the canyon, in search of the perfect tree.

"Your great, great grandpa Kammer was a tall, strong man with a heart so big, they said it spread out all across the valley here," Poppa started as he spread his arms out wide, pointing in both directions towards the north and south of the valley. The girls all giggled and Nikola reached up to hang onto one of Poppa's arms. He swung her back and forth a couple of times before she slid down and ran back over to Momma to walk beside her on their journey. "Then your great grandpa Kammer continued the tradition with great grandma Kammer and their 4 children; followed by your grandpa and grandma Kammer and their 6 children. Each year, always in search of that perfect Christmas tree." "Did they always find a perfect tree, Poppa?" Lucy asked. "Did they ever, Lucy!" Poppa quickly answered, and it took all 6 children to carry the tree back home, out of this very same canyon!" The girls all giggled again and began singing more Christmas songs as they continued their own search for the perfect Christmas tree.

When the Kammer family reached the first landing area on the west side of the mountain just at the entrance to the canyon, Poppa stopped and turned to look over the valley. This was one of his favorite spots to take a break or to have lunch when Izrael and Alex K. worked the ranch. Poppa paused a good long while, then turned back to the family who had stopped to watch him, smiled, and said, "Well, what are you waiting for? Go find that perfect tree, kids!" Everyone started running, or tried to run, in the snow and spread out looking at trees. Now and then one of the girls would yell out, "I found it, I found it" only to discover the tree was too small, or not full enough on one side or the other. Momma was the one to find the perfect tree this year. It truly was perfect. The branches fanned out as if they were bragging on how full and beautiful, they were, and the top of the tree shot out perfectly, just waiting to hold a star on its tip. Each side of the tree was full, and the color was the perfect shade of green that a Christmas tree should be. When Momma pointed it out, everyone gasped. It was perfect.

As the family prepared to take the tree back home, Izrael exclaimed, "How many children will this tree need to help carry it home?" Everyone laughed, except Poppa. He turned to Iz and said, "Just one, and Poppa too." As the Kammer family headed out of the canyon and back down the hill the younger girls began singing again; this time *"Frosty the Snowman"* was the song of choice. As the singing got louder and louder, Izrael wondered if everyone in the valley could hear them, but he didn't care. He loved how happy he felt at that moment, and he wanted to keep these moments alive forever.

Once everyone had dried off and warmed up, it was time for dinner. It was amazing how quickly Momma could pull a meal together. After dinner the children all pulled out the decorations and began decorating the most perfect Christmas tree. They didn't stay at it too long, as they were tired from the tree hunting excursion and decided they would finish the next day. All the girls had gone to bed by the time Izrael could get his turn in the bathroom and get ready for bed himself. He was on his way to his bed when he heard his parents' voices. Their voices were hushed which always made Izrael want to know what they were saying so he stepped in closer towards the family room.

Momma and Poppa were sitting in their comfortable chairs, both facing the partially decorated perfect Christmas tree. Momma sniffled a little and Iz could see she was holding a hankie. He wondered if she had been crying. Poppa was doing most of the talking when Izrael got close enough to hear. What he heard next stunned him. Poppa was talking about his parents, Grandma and Grandpa Kammer. He listened closer. Poppa then said, "You always wanted to know my daddy's secret. Why didn't you just ask me back then?" Momma sniffled again and responded, "It wasn't my place to ask. We weren't even married yet and it was clear that something terrible had just happened." "Yes, that is very true, it was terrible," Poppa answered slowly. Izrael wondered to himself what could have been so terrible!

Poppa kept talking, "Her name was Abigail June, and that is how she introduced herself that day." (What day, Izrael questioned to himself?) "She was so tall and thin, and her head was pointy!" Poppa continued. "Alex K.!" Momma exclaimed, "That's not very nice. But I did notice that too!" The two giggled quietly. Then they were suddenly very serious. Izrael leaned in closer. Their voices were too quiet, he could hardly hear them. He wasn't sure but he thought he heard Poppa say, "She claimed to be my half-sister, Suzanah!" "What?" was all Izrael heard Momma say. Then silence, a silence that seemed to last forever, so long that Iz finally stepped back and quietly made his way to his bed. He laid down but didn't fall asleep for a while. He kept wondering if this person, Abigail June, was really Poppa's half-sister. Grandpa Frank Kammer had another daughter? What about Grandma Rebekah Kammer? How did it impact her? Who was this Abigail June's mother? Izrael had so many questions, but he couldn't ask Momma or Poppa

"Christmas Prep"

because then they would know he was listening, and it was a rule in the family not to eavesdrop on someone else's conversations. The children had always been told that if they were intended to know something, they would be told. Otherwise, they were taught not to ask. Izrael realized he might not ever know the truth. What he didn't realize then was that there was another truth he would soon have to face himself. Izrael wrote in his journal until he fell asleep.

CHAPTER 16

"SWEET MEMORIES"

Izrael woke early the next morning; it was still dark, so he stayed in bed longer than usual. His mind was racing the moment he awoke. He couldn't stop thinking about his grandparents. Iz thought about all the memories playing outside under the big cherry trees that were still making the sweetest cherries anyone ever tasted, at least anyone in the valley. Neighbors often stopped by to visit conveniently at the time the cherries were ripe and ready to pick. No one was ever upset by this because there were too many cherries on the large trees for just one family. Izrael remembered Grandma Kammer handing baskets to his older sisters, Lucy, and Cilla, so they could climb up the ladders and pick the cherries up higher. Izrael was too small to climb the ladder but that never stopped him from begging Grandma K to let him. She would lean over and scoop Iz into her arms while laughing the most perfect grandma laugh, squeeze him, and say, "one day soon enough, sweet little Iz, one day soon." Izrael would giggle and lean into her shoulder. He remembered clearly how she smelled. It was the perfect combination of homemade breads and sweet cherries. Izrael loved his grandma so much.

The memories made Izrael sad this cold winter morning. As he rolled over to his side he began to think back and tried to find anything in his memory that would have anything to do with another aunt being in the family, who no one ever talked about now. He couldn't remember anything, but as he lay thinking he dozed back to sleep and dreamed about being in the house with Grandma and Grandpa Kammer. They were sitting in their comfortable chairs, which still sat in the same room, in the same house where Izrael and his family lived, and where his parents sat now. They were talking quietly, in whispers. In his dream, Izrael tried to ask them what they were talking about, but his voice would not speak, even though he moved his lips.

When Izrael awoke from the dream he felt uneasy, as the image of his grandparents in their chairs was the same image as he had seen his parents the night before. And they were whispering too. The similarity made Izrael shiver. He knew somehow there was a connection, but he did not know what it was, not yet he thought to himself. Then as he rolled back over again to sit up, he decided he would find out what the secrets were all about and the best way to do that was to search the house, and the property for clues.

After the breakfast and morning chores were finished, Izrael went to the family room to pull out the old photo albums. Momma caught a glimpse of him as he walked into the room and asked what he was looking for. "I just want to look at a few family pictures, is that okay, Momma?" "Oh, of course, Iz, you go right ahead, son."

He pulled out the oldest albums first. The pictures of Grandma and Grandpa Kammer sitting out on the front porch made Izrael sigh. The house looked different back then. The porch was smaller and only held two chairs and a pile of firewood. Poppa had extended the porch after Grandpa Kammer passed the house and the property to his son. Being the only son of Frank and Rebekah Kammer, Alex K. was the heir to the property, and the house. His sisters all understood; it was the way men handled property ownership in the family.

Alex K.'s oldest sister, Karina, moved Grandpa and Grandma Kammer to her house to care for them once they were not able to care for themselves. "Aunt K" and her husband's home was on the other side of the tallest mountain from where Alex K and his family now lived.

Izrael remembered the day his grandparents left their home. It was a sad day. He had never seen them cry, but that day they cried. Everyone did, but everyone knew it was the best thing for them. Izrael hugged Grandma Kammer tightly, looked up into her eyes and promised he would go visit her. Many years had passed since that day, and he had still not gone to visit. It was a long and hard drive up and around the mountain. The roads were windy and narrow, and Poppa always told Izrael and his sisters it was too dangerous. Izrael felt his eyes moisten. He missed his grandparents so very much.

Now there was even more reason to go visit. Izrael found himself wanting to know more about Poppa's secret half-sister. One day, he thought to himself, one day.

CHAPTER 17

"A CLUE"

The days leading up to Christmas day were full of decorating, baking, whispering and giggling. There certainly was a more magical feel in the air. Izrael loved these days. He never wanted them to go away. They always seemed to go by quickly. This year Izrael spent more time than usual continuing to think about his grandparents, on the other side of the mountain, and to explore for clues, everywhere he went, whether in the house or outside.

Even with the bitter cold winter winds blowing through the valley, Izrael and Mindee ventured out every afternoon, into the canyon. He couldn't shake the feeling that there were clues out there somewhere and he was determined to find them.

On this particularly cold day, Mindee was moving along at a steady pace, pausing here and there to let a cold burst of wind settle down. It was during one of those pauses that Izrael spotted something shiny, glimmering against the sunlight, on the ground just ahead. He shook his head and blinked a couple of times wondering if it was just the cold wind on his cheeks making him see things, but it was still there, and it seemed to shine brighter the closer they got. Izrael slid off Mindee and slowly stepped towards the shiny object. It appeared to be something metal mostly covered in snow and dirt. Izrael reached down to pick it up and realized there was more to it and the rest of it was under more dirt. Izrael turned back to Mindee, to his day pack that hung off the saddle. Inside he had a small shovel. Izrael pulled it out and went straight to work digging around the shiny metal object. As he dug, he could feel the side of the object and noticed it went down several inches. The ground was cold, covered in snow, and hard to shovel but Izrael was determined. He dug and dug until finally the ground began to give. As Izrael pushed the hard pieces of dirt to the side he realized what he was digging up. It was a binder of some sort, like a book with a shiny metal clip on the side of it. It appeared to be locked. Finally, the whole object came out of the ground. Izrael stared quietly at the book. It was dark and dingy from being in the dirt and the lock looked rusty and old. He wondered what kind of book it might be. Izrael quickly brushed more of the dirt off the sides and stuffed the book into his day pack and set it back on Mindee's side saddle.

 Izrael hopped back onto Mindee's back and slowly pulled on her reigns. They wandered around the area deep in the canyon, where they had found the book, for a while longer. Izrael looked out over the property, noticing how the wind made the tall weeds bend as if they were showing reverence to the power of the wind. Izrael sat on Mindee for a long time watching the weeds. His mind wandered to memories of his grandparents dancing in the weeds together, arm in arm laughing and sometimes even falling down in the weeds. Even as a little boy, Iz thought it was so special to see them happy like that. His mind wandered then to Carolina and the harsh way she had left the valley. The peacefulness of the moment disappeared quickly, and Izrael felt a definite switch in his thoughts, from love to an almost fear of what could have happened if Carolina and her mother had stayed in the valley? What if they had come to talk with Momma and Poppa? How would everything be right now? Iz shuddered at the thoughts and even let out a whistle which startled Mindee who had been grazing quietly.

The clouds were dipping into the valley from up above the horizon which usually meant a storm was brewing. Izrael patted the day pack on Mindee's side and remembered he would have a special time of reading this evening. He felt excited to see what was in the book, or diary was more what it looked like. Whose diary was it? Who would have buried it? Why? So many questions. So many secrets. Were there really secrets in the canyon, on the Kammer property? If there were, Izrael was determined to uncover them. The unknown of those secrets made him a little nervous, but he would find out the truth, one way or another.

Dinner and the evening routine came and went without incident. Izrael excused himself as quickly as he could after things were put away and the bathroom routine had rolled around to his turn. He wanted to get in bed early and spend time reading. He had brought the day pack in earlier and put it in his room so nothing would happen to it. Izrael stopped in his bedroom to get his things and noticed the day pack was not where he had left it. He felt a sudden panic and then heard giggling. It was Nikola giggling in the next bedroom. Izrael rushed over and found her sitting on the floor holding his day pack. "I scared you, didn't I, Iz?" as she giggled again even louder. "Hey, give that to me, Nik!" Izrael blurted out as he dove into the room. "I was just playing with you, Iz, I'm sorry," as she jumped up to give Izrael his pack. She hugged him quickly around his waist and Izrael softened, "It's okay Nikola, you just surprised me," and he kissed her cheek lightly. Izrael loved his little sisters so much. He could never be angry with them. They were his little lights of hope and enjoyment in his world. He thanked God every day for the two of them.

Finally, Izrael was alone in his room. He hurried into bed and covered himself up with the old, beat-up diary under the covers with him. He had managed to rub off the loose dirt while he settled Mindee into her corral for the night, earlier that evening. Now at least the dirt wasn't falling off or making everything else dusty. Izrael remembered that the lock was made of metal and he hoped he would be able to open it. Thankfully, it just fell loose when he pushed up on the latch. It seemed to be opening for him, welcoming him into the past, and that is exactly what happened next.

CHAPTER 18

"HANDWRITINGS"

The diary was full of writings by Izrael's Grandpa Kammer. As soon as the pages opened, he knew it was his grandpa's handwriting. Iz and Grandpa K, as the grandchildren lovingly referred to him, used to sit by the lamplight in the evenings and talk about handwriting skills. Grandpa K would make Izrael practice his penmanship and talked to him often about the importance of handwriting being legible. Izrael sometimes giggled when Grandpa K said this, but Grandpa K never let up; he said, "what your handwriting represents is who you are as a man, Izrael, and it will one day be one of the most important things about you, son." Izrael promised Grandpa K he would always remember, and he tried to sit and practice even now that Grandpa and Grandma K were living far over the mountain.

The diary took Izrael far into Grandpa K's past. He had started writing when he was about the same age that Izrael was now which explained why it looked so old and beat up, not to mention the fact that it had been buried in the dirt, up in the canyon. Izrael wondered quickly again why it had been buried but he kept reading.

The words Grandpa K used to describe the Kammer property were words Izrael thought and said often himself. He described it as "the place that made his heartbeat faster" and "the majestic mountains called out" to him. He wrote about his daily trips into the canyon and how he felt after he came back down to the house. Several times Izrael stopped reading and almost said out loud, "I've said that before!" It was a wonderful time of reading special thoughts and moments from Grandpa K. Izrael felt refreshed and at peace while he read. So many quick notes, so many thoughts that made Izrael feel closer to Grandpa K than he had felt in several years.

The night had swept by while Izrael read. He did not realize it was well past midnight, but he couldn't stop reading. Then suddenly the words in the diary changed. There seemed to be long breaks in the dates when Grandpa K had written and when he did write something, Izrael could almost feel Grandpa K's anger. Izrael began to feel anxious, and a little frightened.

At this point in the diary, Grandpa K was much older than Izrael's current age. He often referred to someone as "that woman" which was then followed by something she had done. It was confusing to read. Izrael was having trouble understanding who the woman could be and what kinds of things she had done to get Grandpa K so upset. The diary never did explain any of it. At one point in the diary, Grandpa K made a note that had been scratched over multiple times. It was apparent he did not want anyone to be able to read it. Izrael held his lamp behind the paper but still couldn't see what it said. He wondered to himself if he might be able to read it once it was daylight.

Izrael read until he could keep his eyes open no longer. He fell asleep holding the diary. The secrets, the messages written inside still a mystery.

CHAPTER 19

"GRANDPA K"

The long winter days crept by and seemed to be slower than any other time of year. The mornings were always cold but the warm fire in the wood burning stoves were quick to warm up the family. Everyone pitched in to keep the house warm. If one of two stoves' fires were getting low, whoever noticed it would add a log. This was a lesson each of the Kammer children were taught as soon as they were old enough to safely add to the fire.

The clouds that had rolled in the day before stayed and there was more snow on the ground to prove it. The younger girls talked about building a snowman while the two older girls talked about working on their projects indoors. Izrael knew that at one point in the day, Lucy and Cilla would bundle up Phina and Nika and take them out to play.

Iz had other plans. He wanted to keep reading the diary, but he wasn't sure where he would be able to read without anyone asking him what he was reading. He knew if he stayed in his room, Momma would think he was sick, and if he sat in the kitchen, everyone would see the diary and want to know what it was. He thought and thought, then finally decided he could sit behind the Christmas tree. There was just enough room for one person and the light from the window was enough for reading. Izrael then grabbed one of his schoolbooks and put the diary inside the book and sat behind the tree. At one point Poppa walked by, looked over towards Izrael and then turned and went the other way. It was only a few more days until Christmas and the harsh winters kept Poppa working indoors. He always had a project or two going and was ready to repair anything that broke. Momma enjoyed having him inside during the winter, as he kept up with the projects, and they always enjoyed chatting with each other.

The timing was perfect for Iz to focus on the diary. He had fallen asleep the night before, confused by the kinds of notes Grandpa K had written. It took him a little while to find where he had last read.

The notes were short and choppy. One note clearly said, "Women are no good!!!" Izrael kept reading. By the time he read all the short notes by Grandpa K, Iz had begun to piece together that there was a woman in Grandpa K's life who had been a friend of Grandpa K, but their friendship didn't last. Izrael wondered what her name was because Grandpa K only referred to her as "that woman" in his notes.

Izrael jumped when he heard Momma call out for everyone to come to the table for lunch. He had gotten about halfway through the diary at this point and still did not know who "that woman" was. "I hope I figure this out after lunch," Izrael thought as he crawled out of his quiet spot behind the Christmas tree and hurried to the kitchen.

During lunch Poppa announced he had something he wanted to tell the family. It was about Grandpa K, he said. Izrael's stomach jumped and flipped inside. After reading so much about Grandpa K for the last day and a half, he felt so close to him. "I'm afraid Grandpa K is very sick, kids," Poppa started. "We received a letter in the mail from your aunt saying he is not well. I am worried about him." Lucy and Cilla grabbed each other's hands and began to sniffle. They both had grown up very close to Grandpa and Grandma K.

Izrael sat up straight and said, "I want to go see Grandpa K, can we go, Poppa?" Poppa leaned back in his chair, tipping the front of the chair while balancing on the back legs. He rubbed his chin a few times before answering, "We will see Izrael. The roads are not good over those mountains and the winter conditions makes it even more difficult. Not sure we can drive my old pick up that far." "Can we go by horseback, Poppa? I know Mindee can do it; she is strong and healthy." Poppa rubbed his chin more, "That might work. What do you think, Suzanah? I worry about leaving all my girls here without a man to protect you all." Momma smiled, "I think we can manage, Alex; besides, my brothers live nearby, and we can always send for one of them if we get in a bind." "That's true," Poppa replied, "and we can ask them to stop by a few times while we are gone." "Does this mean we are going, Poppa?" Iz asked anxiously, "are we?" "Slow down, there son, slow down. Yes, I do think we better go see Grandpa K, but we need at least one day to prepare the animals and make plans for your uncles to check on the girls while we are gone." "That sounds fair," Iz answered quickly, "I'll go pack!" and off Speedy Iz ran to his bedroom to pack a few sets of clothes for the trip.

Izrael could hardly contain himself, he was so excited for the trip. He knew it would be long and bitterly cold, but he didn't care. He was anxious to check on his grandparents and especially get to talk with Grandpa K about the diary. The diary! Iz knew he needed to make sure he took the diary with him. He wondered if anyone would be upset if they found out he had it? For now, Iz decided he would not tell anyone. It would be a secret, until the right time, if ever.

CHAPTER 20

"BITTER COLD"

Alex K and Iz spent the next day working with the animals, checking fence lines, and making sure there were no problems on the ranch for Suzanah to manage while they were gone. Every now and then Iz heard Poppa mumbling to himself. Izrael knew not to ask what Poppa was saying because he had heard him mumble quietly many times before. Iz knew Poppa was praying. He often saw Poppa down on one knee with his hat in one hand and his other hand holding his head as he prayed for something or someone. Izrael never knew who or what Poppa prayed for, but he knew Poppa was good at praying because the ranch and the animals on it was the best-looking land in all the valley.

The following day came quickly. Poppa was up before Izrael, as usual, but not too far ahead of Iz. Izrael was excited and a little nervous to start their journey. Momma, Lucy, and Priscilla had prepared plenty of food and packed it all tightly to keep the food fresh during the journey. Poppa estimated it to be a 2-day trip there and 2 days back. They would stay 1 day and 1 night with the family before returning home. It worried Poppa to leave the ranch even 1 day so this was a difficult decision to make such a long journey.

The morning was, as expected, bitter cold. The air was still, no winds to slow them down. Poppa led the way and stopped to remind Iz they would take advantage of the weather and only make stops when absolutely necessary, "It better be an emergency or we won't be stopping, understood?" "Yes, sir, I understand," Iz quickly answered Poppa with a serious and determined look in his eyes. Poppa noticed his determination and said, "Good deal, let's keep moving."

As the two began climbing the side of the mountain they were seeing up close what they looked at every day from the ranch. Izrael realized how similar the terrain was to their property, only much less traveled, making it more challenging to find the road and make their way around the mountain. Izrael noticed spots of snow here and there from previous storms. They trudged along at a fair pace, keeping their chins tucked in to help keep them warm. They had layered their clothing and even had layers of gloves to help prevent frostbite. No turning back now. They didn't stop until nearly supper time. They were both very hungry, cold, and tired. Poppa built a small fire while Iz pulled out some of the prepared food which they ate quickly before laying their bed rolls in the frozen clay. It would be dark soon and all they could do in the dark was sleep which came easily after the long hard day of travel.

The sun woke them in the morning. It felt good warming their faces while the rest of their bodies were buried in layers of coverings. Izrael was surprised at how warm he was. Poppa knew what he was doing and how to survive the cold outdoors. They moved from their bed rolls to breakfast and back on the horses very fast, to keep from noticing the cold too

"Bitter Cold"

much. Momma's boiled eggs and homemade rolls were a quick fix for their hunger. They were thankful for the sunny day and no clouds in sight which meant an easier ride than if any moisture was in the air. Chins tucked low, layers on their bodies and strong horses to carry them through the day. Poppa was pleased with their trip so far.

Alex K and Izrael managed to arrive at Alex K's sister's home before dark. Aunt K, as Iz and his sisters lovingly referred to Alex K's older sister, Karina Kammer, greeted them warmly at the door. Aunt K had married young, and her husband died in an accident which no one ever talked about. Iz felt sorry for Aunt K and had so much love for her, for the way she loved his Grandpa and Grandma K.

Aunt K immediately began pulling off their cold jackets and hats and gloves and barking out orders how and where to get warmed up and were they hungry and all the wonderful smells in her house. Izrael felt warm inside the minute they walked in. Aunt K had always been Izrael's favorite aunt and this evening sealed that even more.

"How's Dad?" Alex K broke up the happy greeting. Aunt K immediately changed. Her face became serious and sad and the corners of her eyes moistened. "It's not good, Alex, he's very weak." "Can we see him?" Alex responded quickly. "Of course, follow me, this way," was Aunt K's quiet answer. Izrael and Alex K walked slowly behind Aunt K, as if anticipating the worst. The hesitation seemed to collide with the anticipation of not seeing Grandpa K for so long. Before they entered Grandpa and Grandma K's bedroom, Iz heard sniffling. He thought it might be Grandma K, and he was right. She was seated on the far side of the bed from where they entered and looked up as soon as they walked in the room. Grandma K stood quickly and with her arms outstretched hurried over to them, taking them both in her warm and loving arms. She began to softly sob as she buried her head into Poppa's shoulder. The three stood trembling together, no one saying anything, just holding each other.

    Finally, Grandma K pulled back and looked at both Iz and Alex in the eyes, saying without words, thank you for coming! Alex K pulled out his hankie and wiped his eyes. He then slowly walked over to the bed where Grandpa K was sleeping. Izrael hadn't moved. He watched from Grandma K's side as Poppa softly touched his father's arm. Silence. It seemed to invade everything.

CHAPTER 21

"A PRECIOUS LIFE"

The silence lingered, and it seemed like hours before anyone spoke. It was Grandma K who finally said, "He knows you are both here. He's been waiting for you." Iz turned to his Grandma K who pulled him in closer and continued, "the love he has for you boys is so very deep. I hope you know that." Then Izrael heard what he never thought he would hear, sobs coming from his own father. Poppa was sobbing as he laid his head on the side of the bed, near Grandpa K's right arm. "I love you Pop, I hope you know, I love you," Alex K said between his sobs. Izrael could no longer hold back his own tears. They rushed freely down his cheeks as he leaned into Grandma K's shoulder.

The three had not realized that Aunt K had joined them until her sobs joined in with the others. She finally spoke and said, "Let's take a minute to catch our breath, shall we? I have hot soup and cornbread ready. It will give us the strength we need to face the next hours." One by one they each turned to follow Aunt K, except Grandma K. She hesitated and stepped back over to Grandpa K and whispered in his ear, kissed his cheek lightly and then followed them into the kitchen. In silence they filled their bowls and plates with what seemed to be the most delicious meal Izrael had ever tasted. He never compared anyone else's cooking to his own Momma's cooking but right now, in this moment, his stomach was grateful. He felt grateful for the family he was born into. He felt thankful to have the memories he had with Grandpa K, and he was so very, very thankful to be there with him and Grandma K for this night.

As the 4 ate quietly, they could hear Grandpa K breathing while he slept. It was a comfort to hear his breath, as if he were sitting among them, enjoying the tastes. When they finished eating Aunt K began picking up the dishes and Izrael was about to stand to help when Grandma K turned to Poppa and firmly said, "It's time to forgive him, Alexander Shane," in the tone only Grandma K could use with Poppa. Poppa looked straight into her eyes and said, "I don't know how, Momma." Silence invaded again as Grandma K laid her hand over her son's hand and closed her eyes. Her lips were moving but there was no sound. Izrael knew she was praying. So did Poppa. Aunt K had stopped moving around the kitchen and sat down next to Izrael. She leaned towards Iz and said, "No worries, Iz, everything will be okay." Izrael looked down quickly and waited quietly for the next words. What he heard shocked him, and his mind raced back to the diary and "that woman!" Could this be about her?

CHAPTER 22

"TRUTH REVEALED"

"It was a very long time ago, Alexander," Grandma K began. "He was a young lad and did not know better. Some of the friends your Pop had when he was young were not the best kind of folk. They teased him a lot. They made him feel less of man than they were, and he was so prideful then; he still is in fact, to this day. He was in high school when a new family moved into the valley. They had one child, a daughter, who was a little younger than your Pop. The young lady was not very attractive, and she was loud. On her first day at the high school, she announced to anyone who would listen that she was looking for her future husband and that was the only reason she was in school. She bragged about her bad grades and said her only goal in life was to get married and have children."

"What?" Izrael gasped, for a few reasons. Poppa looked up quickly and gave Izrael a look that Izrael understood well, as he had seen it many times. He knew not to say another word, but to just sit quietly.

Grandma K continued, "the young lady flirted and teased any boy who would give her even a little bit of attention. No one talked about things like that back then. If she managed to be alone with a boy, no one knew. Even the boys didn't talk about it with each other. It was a tense time at Forrest Lane High."

When Grandma K said the name of the school, Izrael flinched a little, almost forgetting that Grandpa K had attended the same school Iz attends now. He didn't speak or make a sound though, not wanting to interrupt Grandma K's story; a story that was beginning to make Izrael more and more uneasy.

"That was Grandpa K's senior year," Grandma K continued. "After graduation he poured himself into the ranch that his father had taught and prepared him to manage. That was the end of things with that young lady, or so everyone thought."

Grandma quickly added how she and Grandpa K had met later and what a romantic, loving relationship they had shared as Grandpa K courted her and ultimately asked her to be his wife. They were married at the Kammer ranch and raised their family happily together.

Grandma became quiet again. This time Poppa started talking, "Until Abigail Jane showed up! She showed up out of the blue with all her lies and almost ruined my own wedding plans, Momma!" Grandma touched the edges of her eyes with her tissue and spoke softly, almost too softly to be heard, and said, "Yes, Alexander, she did show up and she nearly ruined a lot more than your wedding plans. She claimed to be your Pop's illegitimate daughter!"

"What?" Izrael again interrupted with another knee-jerk response. This time Poppa didn't scold Iz but only continued looking at his momma with a sadness in his eyes. "Momma, the sound of your scream raced up that mountain and into the canyon that day! Suzanah and I had gone for a stroll and when we heard your screams we came running as fast as we could, I even left Suzanah behind me trying to keep up. I was so upset how Pop hurt you, Momma. Forgiveness is not that easy."

What Grandma K said next stopped everyone.

"She lied, Alexander." Poppa stood up, brushed his hair back with his hand like he did when he was anxious and said, "How can you say that after all these years, how would you know if she was lying, Momma? Did she tell you that?" "No, son, she did not, your Pop did."

At that very moment a sound came from the bedroom where Grandpa K was sleeping. Izrael would never forget that sound, like a rushing wind from the north going up into the canyon. Grandma K stopped talking; they all were frozen, then they seemed to jump to their feet in unison and ran to the bedroom.

Grandpa K was awake! He was looking around and coughing, seeming to not know where he was. As soon as he saw Grandma K he relaxed. His eyes opened wide and filled quickly with tears at the sight of his son and grandson entering the room. He reached his arm towards Alex K and Izrael. They both hurried to the bedside. Now everyone was crying. It was a bittersweet reunion.

CHAPTER 23

"THE TALK"

No one spoke for a very long time. The relief of just being together was enough. More than two hours had passed, as they all sat together, very near Grandpa K's bed. Aunt K had brought in a few of the chairs from the kitchen table, so everyone had a place near the bed. Once Grandpa K had sipped some water and his breathing was back to a calm pace, he began to speak. His voice was weak from having been asleep for so long, but his determination was strong. He started, "I knew you boys would come. The Kammer men may be stubborn, but we stick together." As Grandpa K began to laugh it quickly turned into coughing and both Grandma K and Aunt K jumped to assist him. "Oh, stop hovering, I haven't died yet!" Everyone chuckled a little which helped calm the tension a bit more.

Grandpa K cleared his throat and rubbed his hand over his head. Izrael could not help but notice the similarity between Grandpa K and Poppa; they both seemed to rub their heads when something was serious.

"Alex, son, are you still here?" "Yes, Pop, I am here," Alex K answered quickly as he reached over to touch his father's hand.

Grandpa K squeezed Alex's hand and breathed a huge sigh, as if he were relieved that his son had not left.

"I'm here, Pop, I'm not leaving," Poppa said firmly. Grandpa K took another big breath. "I've been hard on you, son, and I know you have been angry with me for some time." Alex K began to interrupt but Grandpa K raised his hand as if to say "Stop!" and Alex K stopped. "It's time you know the whole story, son." Everyone seemed to stop breathing, as there was no sound in the room. Even Aunt K's sniffles had stopped.

"I was young and stupid back then," Grandpa K began. "Life was so different than it is now. People helped each other and hard work was expected. They also respected each other. Men respected women in ways that no one had to explain, it was just understood. Many days I could not attend school because the priority was working on the ranch with my dad. Usually, the winter months were when the older boys would go to school because it was too cold to work the land. That's when all the girls chased us boys!" Aunt K giggled softly but quickly stopped when she realized how serious everyone's faces looked. Grandpa K continued, "One of them girls kept chasing me and I did everything I could to ignore her. She was like a stubborn mule and sort of looked like one too!" This time everyone laughed but did not stop listening to every word coming from Grandpa K. "I was bound and determined not to get caught by a girl back then. I wasn't ready for that, and I had big plans to keep working the ranch with my dad and did not have time for any girl. This just made Penelope angrier."

"Penelope?" Izrael blurted out before he could stop himself. No one seemed to notice, as Grandpa K kept talking. "She wanted me to marry her and we had not even graduated from high school yet. I was honest with her. I let her know I was not ready for a wife, nor was I ready to be a husband. She cried and carried on and promised me she would get even with me for rejecting her. Well, that she did. She told everyone in the valley that I had forced myself on her and she was pregnant with my child!" Alex K leaned back in his chair and said, "Oh, Abigail June!" "None of it was true, not a word!" exclaimed Grandpa K. "Then why did she show up at the ranch that day introducing herself as your illegitimate daughter, Pop, why?" Alex quickly shot back to Grandpa K. Silence again, then Grandpa K sat as high as he could, looked Alex K straight in the eyes and as clearly as he could say it, shot back, "She lied to everyone, Alex! I never had any kind of relations with that lying fool and the guy who did would not fess up."

Those words seemed to wear Grandpa K out, as he leaned back against the pillow, took a deep breath, and closed his eyes. Grandma K stood up and leaned over him whispering quietly. Izrael imagined she was trying to keep him calm. No one else spoke. The five sat quietly again. It had gotten late. Finally Aunt K got up and began straightening things up in the room. She turned towards Izrael and said, "Grandpa K has had a hard day. He needs his rest now." Izrael stood to prepare to leave the room when Grandpa K opened his eyes again and this time looked at Iz. He called him over to his side. Izrael hurried over to the side of the bed where Grandma K stood. She stepped aside to let Iz move in closer. Grandpa K reached for Izrael's arm, squeezed him tightly and said, "Don't ever let anything like this happen to you, Izrael. You need to break the curse! Do you understand me?" Izrael could hardly believe what he was hearing but very quickly responded with, "Yes, sir, I understand, sir!" With that, Grandpa K closed his eyes and took his last breath. Izrael realized he had made a promise to his grandpa that had potential to be a hard promise to keep.

The three stood silently weeping. They stayed in the room for a good while until Aunt K finally said she would make a phone call. Alex K and Izrael stood on both sides of Grandpa K when he stopped breathing. They had not made eye contact with each other until Grandma K asked if they were okay. They looked up at each other and Izrael was sure he heard Poppa say, "I have a bad feeling about that girl, Izrael," like he had said the day Izrael had spoken to Poppa about Carolina, but Poppa's lips hadn't moved. He was standing still, looking at Izrael, as a slow tear slid down the side of his face. Izrael would never forget this moment, nor this evening with Grandpa K.

Izrael realized he never got to ask Grandpa K about the diary he had found, but it turned out he did not need to ask. The stories were told to them in that room that night, around Grandpa K's bed. That was all that needed to be said. The eeriness of similarity between Penelope and Carolina made Izrael's skin crawl. He had written a few things in his own journal that were like what Grandpa K had written, even before he found the diary. Izrael feared writing too much, in case one day someone found his writings and learned his own secrets.

CHAPTER 24

"THE LONG RIDE HOME"

People were buried soon after they died, and Grandpa K's funeral was a short one. Izrael felt a little uneasy about how fast it all happened, but Grandma K had explained they had to do it quickly before the body began to decompose. Izrael did not like the idea of his Grandpa's body doing that so he nodded and thanked her for explaining.

The day following the funeral Alex K and Izrael began the two-day journey home, over the mountain, again in the bitter cold. The two did not talk much the first day, both deep in their grief. On the second day as they reached their side of the mountain, Alex K began to share with Izrael. He started out by affirming what Grandpa K had told them, and to add how relieved he was to finally know the truth. "I've been angry with your Grandpa K for a long time, Izrael. There were times I was downright mean about it too. I am feeling sorry for having held that anger for so long. If I had just listened when he tried to talk with me about it, but I never let him!" Izrael didn't know what to say, so he stayed silent. Poppa went on, "I believed Abigail June when I heard her words, and I didn't believe my own Pop. But things are going to change. I am going to call that

Abigail June and let her know we know the truth, Iz. I have to do this for Grandpa K. I just have to."

Izrael nodded to his Poppa, to show he understood. That was the end of that discussion. Izrael had seen another side of his Poppa, and for the first time he was beginning to understand where Poppa's anger had come from. Izrael wondered if Poppa was beginning to soften; being with Grandpa K when he took his last breath made a huge impact on both Kammer men. The remainder of the trip was focused on staying warm and how much longer before they would arrive home. The horses did well but the ground was cold, and the sun didn't stay out long enough. Poppa had commented that a storm was likely coming so they had better hurry and not rest too long.

When they finally arrived home, Izrael had never felt more relieved and more emotional than he did when he saw Momma at the door holding two warm blankets, ready to welcome her men home. As he stepped in and felt the warmth of the blanket and the love from Momma, Izrael just melted. He stood crying in Momma's arms and she wept with him, stroking his back and softly saying, "It's going to be okay, son, you're home, everything is okay."

It was so good to be home. Even Poppa seemed relaxed and at ease after the cold, hard trip. He allowed a couple of days for he and Iz to rest, staying near the house and mostly inside due to the huge snowstorm he had predicted. The storm dumped several inches of new snow on the ground overnight, the night they arrived home. The whole family continued to grieve for Grandpa K, as they kept a candle burning in his honor for several days. They felt sad about their loss but thankful for the years and memories. Most of their conversations were focused on stories each had about Grandpa K. Izrael wondered if Poppa had told Momma about Grandpa K's last words, but never felt comfortable enough to ask so he stayed quiet about it, knowing Poppa would handle it the way he chose to.

Later in the week, as the snow started to melt, Poppa and Izrael were working outside, fixing a post along a fence line near the house, when they heard Momma ringing the bell on the porch. Usually the bell meant dinner was almost ready and they needed to start wrapping things up, but it was way too early for dinner. This meant only one thing, Momma needed Poppa to come to the house quickly. They grabbed their tools and hurried back down the hill. As they dropped their bags and tools on the porch, Izrael could hear another voice coming from inside the house. The voice was loud and demanding.

Poppa walked in first and slowed his steps enough that Izrael nearly bumped into Poppa as he stepped through the doorway. There was a tall and strong looking woman standing in the entryway. She seemed to be yelling at Momma, whose face was flushed and a little red around her brow, the way it got when Momma was upset. Izrael became quickly concerned and stood beside Poppa, between he and Momma, as if he could shield Momma from this intruder.

From the corner of his eye Izrael saw his sisters all standing close to each other at the entryway to the kitchen. Poppa turned towards them and said, "Lucy, please take your sisters into the family room and play some cards or read some books." "Yes, sir," was all Lucy said in response as she guided her younger sisters out.

"Well, well, that didn't take long, did it?" Poppa said to the tall woman. "Alex, how nice to see you again," the woman responded. "Nothing nice about it!" Poppa shot back. "What is that supposed to mean? Why are you sounding so...," the woman started to answer but Poppa interrupted before she could finish. "Abigail June, you are not welcome here! We know the truth about you and your worthless mother and all I am going to tell you is it's time for you to leave!" So this was Abigail June, Iz thought to himself. She was so very tall and remembering Grandpa K's description of her mother almost made him snicker, but he held back and continued to listen. "The truth has come out, Miss, and we have no family ties with you so it's time you leave."

By this point the woman had started to cry. She looked at Momma with a pleading in her eyes and asked if she could sit. Momma, who was always kind to strangers, nodded as Abigail June sat on a wooden chair near the front door. After dabbing her eyes, she looked up at Poppa and asked if he would tell her what he knew. Poppa had softened his tone a little and pulled up a stool, sitting down hard. Finally, he looked Abigail June in the eyes and said, "My Pop just passed away last week. I was with him; my son and I were there. In his last words he told us what happened between him and your momma." "What did he tell you?" Abigail June asked. Poppa then told her the whole story, everything both Grandpa K and Grandma K had shared with them. It was clear this was all new to Abigail June. When she was able to speak again, she slowly responded, "I am so sorry to have bothered you and your family, Alex. I believed everything my mother told me, and now she is gone too so I cannot go back and address this with her. She passed away a few weeks ago. Thank you for telling me the truth. I won't be back."

Alex K stood up next to Suzanah who had reached out to squeeze Abigail June's arm. She smiled slightly, turned to Izrael, and said, "You have a beautiful mother. You are one lucky young man." Izrael nodded, "Yes, ma'am. I agree, thank you." With that, the woman stepped out the door and out of their lives. Izrael heard his poppa's deep sigh of relief and noticed he had his arm around Momma who had tears in her eyes. "That poor woman," Momma said, "She seems so lonely and so sad."

CHAPTER 25

"MID-WINTER"

The days continued and the Kammer children were soon back at school. The holidays had come to an end, and it was a new year. New opportunities to do good things and Izrael was full of anticipation with his last semester of high school upon him. He felt like things were as they had been before Carolina had shown up at the beginning of his senior year. He was happy again, hanging out with his friends and just being "one of the guys." Life felt so much better!

Speedy Iz, as his friends still called him, and his 3 best friends would meet outside before school started every morning. They stayed near the front steps of the building to be sure not to be late to class. Most mornings one of the boys would be close enough to hold the door open for one of the girls, or the teachers carrying too many books in their arms. Many of the kids called them the 4 doormen, rather than the 4 musketeers as they had been called through the years, for always being together.

The guys supported each other like family. If anyone had need of extra hands at home, they were the first to show up, as long as their own family approved. It was a special bond and Izrael felt especially thankful for his friends after the last few months. It seemed time had stood still, nothing was different. Just the 4 musketeers hanging out and being there for each other.

Many nights, as Izrael said his prayers, he thanked God for his friends and would ask God to never let anything change, to let them be friends forever. He wanted this almost more than anything.

Izrael also prayed for his family. Being so close to the end of his high school education made Izrael a little sad. He wasn't sure what would come, but he knew he wanted to keep working the ranch.

The cold mountain valley winters were always long and hard, and the time between January to March seemed to last longer than 3 months. The ground stayed cold and hard well into April so outdoor work on the ranch was minimal, mainly focused on keeping the animals fed and as warm as possible. Not an easy task for the Kammer men. Iz followed Poppa's lead and stayed close, always ready to head out and face the cold when necessary. Often Iz would think of Grandpa K and his diary, and of him and Poppa braving the cold weather on horseback to see Grandpa K before he died. That diary seemed to have a life of its own, as so much of what was written on those pages continued to live, in Izrael's own life. Iz shook his head as if to tell himself to stop thinking so much and to let those words rest; but would they?

CHAPTER 26

"SPRING"

Hints of spring popped up now and then, but everyone knew there was plenty of cold still to come. Snowstorms rolled in throughout the springtime, just when everyone in the valley was ready to shed their winter coats for lighter weight jackets. The difference with the spring storms was the snow didn't stay long. It usually melted within a day or two, as the sun was warming the ground and everything in it.

Izrael and his little sisters often started their morning walk to school bundled up and had to carry their coats home in the afternoon because it was too warm to wear them. Nikola would whine and try to get Iz to carry her coat, but he insisted she wrap it around her waist and take care of her own belongings. She always listened to her big bubba, smiling and singing while she skipped along the road.

The best part of spring was the excitement and the joy of a new season, fresh and filled with happiness. This spring was especially exciting for Izrael and his classmates; it was their last semester of high school, and they were thrilled to have gotten to this time in their lives. The 22 students in the senior class of Forrest Lane High School could hardly wait. It was all they talked about, even to the point of teachers reminding them if they didn't listen in class and pay attention, they might not graduate! These kinds of threats usually ended with a lot of laughter, knowing the class would stay focused and get their work done. Izrael was determined to finish strong. He knew whatever happened next in his life, he would use everything he had learned in school to make himself a better man.

CHAPTER 27

"ANTICIPATION"

It was only 2 weeks before graduation. The whole class was feeling senioritis. Izrael even started to bug his sisters a little bit, with his nonstop talking about being almost done with high school. Lucy and Cilla reminded him often that he was not the first Kammer to graduate. This only made Iz laugh and get a little more puffed up, as he would say he was the next Kammer man to graduate from Forrest Lane High School. His sisters would giggle and throw a towel or something at Iz and tell him to settle down.

Even in the midst of the excitement, in the midst of the joy, Izrael could not dismiss a feeling of impending doom coming over him. He wasn't sure exactly what it might be, but every time he felt it, Carolina's face and big smile would fill his mind. He would find himself shaking his head, as if to shake her out of his memory, if only he could.

It was in these moments Izrael had the urge to run, into the canyon, and not slow down for anything. Today was one of those days. Once the chores were done and things were quiet with the family, Speedy Iz took off. Suzanah had stepped out onto the porch while Iz started running away from the house.

She stopped and called out to him, "Speedy Iz, be careful up there!" When Izrael heard Momma's voice, he waved his hand. She knew his special wave meant he was okay. Still, she wondered why he had been running into the canyon so often lately. Things were exciting for Izrael right now; so much to look forward to and yet he seemed troubled. Suzanah knew better than to stew over her thoughts and concerns, as she trusted God's hand was over Izrael and He would always cover him, no matter what. She had prayed this for Iz since before he was born. At the time she had two daughters and so wanted a son. Suzanah prayed for a son for Alex K, knowing he would need a son to carry on the family ranch and to be his helper.

Izrael never disappointed Suzanah, not once. She wished she could say the same for Alex K. He never seemed completely satisfied with Izrael and it bothered her so much. All she could see in her son was a kindhearted, loving, and hardworking young man who loved God first, and his family next. Alex K would often say things to Suzanah about Izrael that would cause her heart pain. She never understood why and wanted so badly for him not to talk that way. Suzanah never challenged her husband; she knew better.

Speedy Iz found himself quickly at the top of the first hill. He stopped long enough to take in the view. Looking out over the valley always brought peace to Izrael; he never grew tired of this feeling, nor ever took for granted where he lived and what he saw every single day of his life. At this moment, he had forgotten why he took off running in the first place. He felt such peace and joy, the difficult and frightening thoughts he had at the bottom of the hill had vanished.

The sound of rustling in the bushes invaded Izrael's thoughts and he turned quickly. He caught a glimpse of a bear

"Anticipation"

and her cub climbing up the next part of the hill. Izrael froze to watch. He absolutely loved bears and was thrilled to see them but knew not to startle them or make the momma bear feel threatened. He stayed frozen in place watching and taking in the sight. After horses, bears were Izrael's favorite animal. He had seen quite a few over the years, especially when he and Poppa were working higher on the mountain. They had learned to respect the bears territory and not ever let them fear human presence. It had made for a good relationship, sharing the land with these beautiful creatures.

Once the two were out of sight, Iz pulled his journal out of his back pocket and made notes of the experience. He did not want to forget how special it was to see a momma bear and her cub on the Kammer ranch. As he was jotting down notes, Izrael remembered the poem he had started months before and had been unable to finish. "What should he call it?" Izrael thought to himself. Oh, "The Cowboy!" Iz blurted out loud. "It's a perfect title," he thought. And so he continued...

At night, when work is done, he throws a bed roll in the clay,
His pistol in its' holster, hopes to make it one more day

Oh, the cowboy, the cowboy, the cowboy in me.....
the cowboy

"Yes, the cowboy in me!" Izrael said loudly, up on the side of their mountain, well into the canyon. "That is what I am meant to be and let myself continue to be always." Izrael became quite excited at this revelation. He had been doubting himself, and his abilities, as graduation grew closer and closer. The teachers often asked the seniors, whether one-on-one, or in a group, what their plans were after graduation. Izrael's palms of his hands would break out into a sweat and his heart raced with a feeling of uncertainty. He had not been sure why he felt overwhelmed when he was asked this question.

Today, on the side of the mountain, with his pen and journal full of parchment paper, Iz wrote down his thoughts. He knew without a doubt what he was called to do. He was a cowboy, and he was the next man in line to run and manage Kammer Ranch. He would make his Poppa proud. He would make Momma proud, although he knew in his heart, she was already proud. It always took so much more effort to please Poppa.

Izrael often talked with Poppa about the ranch and his desire to keep working with him but it never seemed as if Poppa believed him. Maybe Izrael had not yet convinced himself. He was certain now, and he could hardly wait to get back down to the house and make this clear to Poppa, and all the family.

When Izrael looked down to close his journal and tuck the pen into the side holder, he saw her name, as if it had popped off the page and was dangling and taunting him. Iz felt his eyes grow wide and his heart race. When he focused on the page the words all pushed together, and he could not read them. Izrael felt panic in that moment. He quickly slammed the journal closed and shoved it into his back pocket while his heart continued racing. "I don't have time for nonsense," Iz said loudly as if he were saying it directly to Carolina, "and I won't let you back in!"

With those thoughts fully inflamed in his mind Speedy Iz flew down the mountainside. As he skirted around wild brush and small pine trees, he could feel some relief. Running always helped his mind and he felt himself begin to slow down to a quick walking pace and finally to his normal pace. When he came out of the upper end of the canyon and could see the Kammer house, Izrael saw Mindee grazing nearby, and ran over to her. The sun had not yet started to drop behind the big mountain to the west. Mindee, as always, showed her excitement to see Iz and they both cheered each other's company in the way they usually did. This time, Iz let out a loud, "Yee-Haw!" After all, he now considered himself a cowboy, and that was how cowboys cheered. This made Izrael laugh to himself. One of the best feelings Izrael had ever known, was in having a horse he loved and who loved him back. Mindee was the very best. He jumped on her bare back and Mindee took off to the north then back south as they zig-zagged their way down the mountain, getting closer and closer to the house.

They slowed down as they approached the corral where Mindee spent her nights. The trough was full of fresh water, and Poppa had set fresh hay inside the corral to coax Mindee in. She needed no coaxing, as the two trotted into the corral. Iz jumped off and turned to reach for Mindee's blanket which he draped over her back to keep her warm overnight. She nudged under Izrael's arm and the two stood in the quiet, letting the other know how much they loved each other. This was another favorite time of the day for Izrael, every single day, and he was excited at the thought of having this to look forward to forever.

CHAPTER 28

"GRADUATION DAY"

The anticipation of graduation had been great for Izrael, and the day had finally come. Izrael awoke that morning with a feeling of excitement and gratitude. He quickly said a prayer of thanks before jumping out of bed and hurrying to get himself ready for the day. This would be a day he would never forget, Iz was sure of it. He hoped to talk with Poppa before the family climbed into Poppa's truck to attend his graduation. He wanted Poppa to know how sure he felt about everything, about his future. He was overjoyed and, yet the feeling of doom kept creeping up inside him. He could feel it start in his gut, working its way up until it hit his throat and nearly made him thrust forward as if he were about to be sick to his stomach. It was a horrible feeling. Again, Izrael shook his head to make it go away. Today was too big of a day to let "feelings" get in his way. He was a man now, a "Real Cowboy" and it was time to act that way and be who he was called to be.

The excitement of the day carried to the rest of the household, as everyone scurried around getting ready for the graduation ceremony which was being held in the high school gym. Iz spent many days and evenings, not to mention weekends, in that gym. He had grown to love playing basketball with his classmates and friends. They were all basketball heroes, as the community called them. Their team had won nearly all their games their senior year and the school and community celebrated the boys, as if they truly were heroes. These were memories Izrael would never forget.

Momma stepped into Izrael's room and caught him looking out the window and asked what he was thinking about. Izrael jumped a little at the sound of Momma's voice to which she giggled but waited for him to reply. "Oh, Momma, so many memories at Forrest Lane! I can't help but feel a little sad for it to be done, but even more excitement for what is to come!" "Yes, Iz, I know. This is a big day for you. We are all so proud of you and all your amazing accomplishments, Izrael!" Momma gave Iz a big hug and a kiss on the cheek. "Thank you, Momma!" Izrael responded, hugging her tightly, feeling so much love and joy at that very moment.

The family ate a quick lunch. The ceremony was scheduled to start at 2:00 p.m., and Iz needed to arrive at least 30 minutes before in order to be in his assigned spot along with his classmates. Poppa always made sure his family was on time to any events they attended. Today was so very important to all the family, and that meant they were early. Iz was the first senior to arrive. He wandered around the gym, remembering highlight moments, feeling nostalgic and praying for his little sisters to have wonderful memories during their years at Forrest Lane. Even though the last few months had some drama, the rest of his memories were just perfect. "Speedy Iz, what are you doing? Come join us!" Iz spun around to find his buddies all smiling ear to ear and waiting for him. Izrael rushed over and the four had a group hug; MJ, Benji, Cliff and Iz, all together, as always. Well, at least for now. Izrael did not realize what was ahead for the four musketeers, none of them did.

The master of ceremonies, otherwise known as Mr. George Fischer, the principal of Forrest Lane High School, broke up the chatter in the gym and pulled everyone together for the ceremony to begin. It was a moment in time that stood still for Izrael Shane Kammer. He could hardly wait to hear his name and walk across the stage. First, Mr. Fischer spoke, then a couple of teachers shared as the 35 mm slide show began. Izrael caught a glimpse of Momma in the crowd, holding her hankie and dabbing her eyes when his photos projected on the screen. The class was lucky to have a slide show, many thanks to the drama teacher who insisted this was an important part of graduation. She was so right, thought Izrael to himself, until he looked up and thought he saw Carolina in the background of one of his pictures. He anxiously looked around and no one seemed to notice it, even Momma didn't change expression. Izrael shook his head, noting the background was blurry and told himself it was his anxiety getting the best of him. He didn't want to think about her, especially today. Iz forced himself to get his attention back on the ceremony. At that moment, he realized that the valedictorian, Emily Mae Jones, was speaking. She began her speech talking about the years with her classmates at Forrest Lane, nearly bringing everyone to tears. Emily Mae was by far the smartest girl in the class, often challenging Iz to step it up and try to beat her out of her spot as valedictorian. Iz knew better not to do so. He had seen her blow up in class many times when someone outsmarted or challenged her.

The greatest moment of the day began; Mr. Fischer stepped back up to the microphone and asked the class to stand. Each of the 22 stood proudly, side-by-side, ready to receive their diplomas. In alphabetical order, each student was called. Each walked to the stage, up the stairs, across to shake hands with Mr. Fischer, then back down the stairs to the other side of the stage and back to their seats.

"Izrael Shane Kammer," it was Izrael's turn, and he never felt prouder. He stepped up to the stage and excitedly shook hands with Mr. Fischer, thanking him for everything. Mr. Fischer smiled as he pried his fingers out of Izrael's hand, laughing and congratulating him the whole time. As he walked across and stepped off the stage, he could hear his sisters all cheering and looked over to see Momma and Poppa hugging each other, smiling, and waving at Iz. He could not remember feeling as good as he did at that moment.

The remainder of the ceremony was wonderful for everyone in attendance. The class stayed around hugging each other until parents gradually pulled their own graduates out to head home for their family celebrations. Izrael was one of the last to leave. Momma, Poppa, and his sisters were all patient, letting him enjoy the time with his friends. As they began to climb into Poppa's pickup, Iz thought he saw a familiar smile. He turned quickly but didn't see it again. Izrael's stomach did a flip, but he felt sure it was just his imagination so he, again, shook it off. Izrael felt a bit uneasy at how much he was "shaking" things off these days, but the happy chatter from his little sisters quickly took those thoughts away. They went on and on about how much fun it was watching Iz, and how happy he looked the whole time.

Momma had started part of dinner early that morning so putting their celebration feast together didn't take long. The girls all helped while Poppa and Izrael sat out on the porch. Since they had been in such a hurry earlier, Iz did not have a chance to talk with Poppa. This now seemed like the perfect time. He began, "Poppa, I've been thinking a lot lately, about the future, and what I really want to do, and all I want is to keep working here on the ranch with you, helping keep the ranch strong and successful, learning from you. I want to be ready when it is time for me to take over. I am ready to be a real cowboy." After a long pause, Poppa finally spoke up, "That's great to hear, Iz. I truly am proud of you, and I am relieved to hear you want to stay around and keep the family business strong. It's what I have always dreamed, for us to work side-by-side and be the Kammer Ranch together. Thank you for telling me this today, Izrael, thank you."

"Let the celebrating continue!" Momma called out, and Izrael nearly knocked over a pot on the porch rushing towards the door to enjoy the amazing meal Momma had prepared for him, complete with her famous biscuits. The biscuits actually had a little curl at the top of them, like her cupcakes always did. "Thank you, Momma! You are the best and you make the most delicious food of anyone in the valley! Everything is delicious!" Momma chuckled and said, "Oh, Iz, you are so much fun to cook for!" She then surprised everyone with fresh baked cherry pies, another favorite of her only son.

CHAPTER 29

"A MAN NOW"

Izrael would never forget that Friday, and the entire graduation celebration. As he awoke the next morning, his mind was flooded with emotions of the day before. He decided it was the best day he had ever experienced. Now that he was no longer in school, he could get busy being a full-time cowboy. He was very excited.

After a quick note in his journal, Izrael got ready for the day, knowing Poppa was already out starting the routine. He felt that would be his next attempt; to be ready earlier and to start the day when Poppa started.

Momma was singing and praising God while working in the kitchen as Izrael walked in. When she heard him, she turned and smiled so big, Iz wondered what was going on. Momma was just so happy, she told him, and so proud of everything. It felt so good to see her happy and Izrael promised himself he would always work to keep his momma happy.

He ate quickly and hurried to catch up with Poppa.

"Well, Izrael Shane, you're a man now," Poppa greeted Iz in a serious tone as he approached. "Yes, sir, I am," Izrael responded confidently. "Do you know what that really means,

Iz?" Poppa continued. Before Iz could answer, Poppa began telling Izrael about his beginnings on the Kammer ranch. Izrael had heard the stories before, but this time felt different. It was as if hearing every part of the story would make or break his future. Izrael felt the pressure Poppa was putting on him. He wondered to himself how much harder Poppa would be on him; Iz would have to stay tough and not let Poppa's comments bother him. It would be challenging. Izrael felt completely ready for the challenge.

Alex K remembered how hard his dad was on him as he was being groomed to take over the ranch. He knew he would need to be the same with Izrael in order for Iz to be prepared and strong enough in many ways, to run Kammer Ranch one day. Alex K also felt different since his father had passed just a few short months before; he wanted Izrael to have a better experience than he had with his father.

"Son, the next couple of years will be hard, and I will push you harder than I ever have before. Are you ready?" he asked Izrael. "Yes, sir, Poppa, I understand why you have to be hard on me and I am ready. I am so excited and happy to be your son at this moment, Poppa, you have to believe me." "Oh, I believe you, son. I just want to be sure you know what is ahead. We will start Monday, looking at the business side of the ranch. I want to be sure you understand everything." "That sounds great, Poppa. Thank you, Poppa!" Izrael responded enthusiastically. Poppa nodded and smiled at Izrael, in the way he did when he was feeling proud and happy. It was a good start, Izrael thought to himself, yes, a very good start.

The rest of the day was spent going through their usual routine with the animals and property lines.

"A Man Now"

That night, as Izrael began getting ready for bed, his mind was racing. What would Poppa teach him first about the business? Would it be hard to understand? Would the math be different than what he had been doing at school? What if he failed; what would Poppa say to him? Izrael began to pray, "Oh, God, help me be successful as a Rancher, as the future owner of Kammer Ranch. Help me to not disappoint Poppa, or Momma." With that, Izrael's eyes moistened, and he drifted quietly to sleep.

CHAPTER 30

"HARD WORK PAYS OFF"

The hard work truly was beginning to pay off. Izrael was recognizing a change in himself. He felt empowered and challenged. These kinds of feelings were new to Izrael. He spent his growing up years feeling like he had to go out of his way to please Poppa and then he never felt he had pleased him. Those kinds of feelings had begun to fade over the next several weeks after graduation.

Iz and Poppa spent every day together throughout the week. Some days were spent hauling hay to the horses and cattle. They dropped the bales in various spots on the property where Poppa wanted them to graze. The spring rains had been good, and they were expecting there to be plenty of grassland for the animals to graze but until then the hay bales helped keep them all in the right fields on the property. Izrael was learning that there had been a strategy to selecting the fields where the horses and cattle would graze. He had never noticed this until his training began and he was fascinated. Iz was also realizing how smart Poppa was; he never knew there would be so much to learn about ranching. Izrael was loving every minute of it.

His nerves about the math Poppa used were quickly calmed, as he realized it was all the same as what he had learned in school. The surprising part was how much Poppa used math on the job. Izrael was guessing it was a daily event for Poppa to take out his pocket notebook he kept with a pen in the top left of his shirts, and scribble numbers then start multiplying and sometimes dividing. Izrael was impressed with Poppa's ability to process the math so quickly. Poppa gave Izrael a notebook and pen to keep in his top left shirt pocket. Izrael accepted the notebook and pen with pride. He knew that meant more to Poppa than just giving him something to write with. It meant he trusted Iz to take notes, to understand the need to write down numbers and to not let himself forget what he had just finished measuring or calculating. All the writing reminded Izrael of Grandpa K and how he had done the same thing with a small notebook and pen in his upper left pocket in his shirts. It was a Kammer man habit, and he was now part of that tradition.

Izrael also remembered Grandpa K's diary he had found buried in the dirt the winter Grandpa K passed away. He would never forget that experience nor the journey to see Grandpa K one more time. Those memories stayed with Iz; they shaped him and encouraged him to keep going and to be the best man he could possibly be.

One morning, as Poppa and Iz were preparing to ride horseback along the fence lines, Izrael's buddies from school showed up. They stopped to say hello to the Kammer family and Momma offered them coffee and biscuits. MJ, Benji and Cliff never turned down Momma's biscuits and made sure she knew they were the best biscuits in the valley. Momma loved Izrael's friends and always enjoyed their visits. All 3 had been working on their own family ranches, since graduation, and had taken the day off to drive into the next community to pick up supplies. They wanted to know if Alex K and Izrael needed anything from town and asked if Izrael wanted to join them.

Izrael expected Poppa to turn them down but was surprised when he agreed. Poppa handed Iz a list of supplies and enough cash to cover the cost plus buy his lunch. After double checking with Poppa and Momma and getting Mindee set to graze while he was gone, Izrael joined his friends for their day together. The trip took about two hours each way, plus the time spent shopping and getting something to eat so they all knew they would not be back until suppertime.

Izrael had not realized how much he missed his buddies until they started down the road. The laughter was likely echoing through the valley as they cruised the dirt roads headed to the main highway. They had the windows down as they began their day off together. MJ was driving, as usual, and the 4 squeezed close to each other in his pickup truck. They each told stories of experiences they had since graduation and working with their dads. Most of the stories were similar to each other, except when Cliff shared about falling into a hole after he and his dad had moved their outhouse. They were all laughing until they cried over that one! The image of Cliff covered in human waste was too much for all of them. Even Cliff laughed, although he was clear to explain that it was not funny at the time. They remembered stories of kids in the valley sneaking onto private property and moving outhouses and the fury heard the next morning when someone fell in. It was an old trick that never seemed to die. Izrael and his friends had never been a part of causing someone to fall into a dark hole like that so hearing about Cliff's experience was even more entertaining. The two-hour drive felt like about 15 minutes. Izrael had not realized how much he needed a day with his buddies.

The foursome worked through their lists, all needing to stop at the same stores, as their lists were similar, being they all worked on family ranches. Momma had asked Iz to look for a jug of honey which he had trouble finding. Finally, they stopped at one of the local markets and he was able to purchase the honey. While they were waiting to pay, MJ saw someone he knew and stepped outside. The other 2 followed him out while Iz finished his purchase. When he stepped outside a dark colored car was pulling away from where his 3 friends were standing in the parking lot. Izrael hurried over and asked who they were talking to. All 3 looked a little pale and no one answered him. Izrael asked again and this time MJ spoke up and told Iz to forget it, she wasn't anyone he knew. "She?" Izrael gasped. "Do you have a girlfriend, MJ?" "What? No, nothing like that, Izrael. She's just someone my family knows from up here. I hadn't seen her in several years and I saw her standing by her car while you were paying so I came out to say hi." Izrael didn't think about it again, at least not for several days.

The rest of their day was uneventful but not without laughter. MJ, Benji, Cliff and Izrael talked and laughed all the way home. MJ dropped Izrael off first, as he had been their last stop before heading out that morning. Iz grabbed his bags and waved as his buddies drove off. It had been a great day.

CHAPTER 31

"MORE LIES"

Izrael spent the rest of the week working with Poppa, learning more about the inner workings of running a ranch. Iz loved every minute of it and soaked up all that he could while he and Poppa worked together. Often times Iz would stop, pull out his notebook and pen, sit on a rock and write down his notes. Poppa smiled watching Iz, remembering when he was younger; always eager to learn and do everything he could to please his own poppa, Grandpa K. Generations continued similar habits.

It was Friday afternoon and usually that meant Alex K and Izrael would quit work a little early to have some family time with Izrael's sisters and Momma. Today was a little different, as they had found a few spots on one of the fence lines that had fallen and that was never a quick fix. Finally, the two started their ride back home, horses loaded and ready for the weekend.

As they rode down the last hill, Poppa spoke up, wondering whose vehicle was parked near the house. Izrael popped his head up, stretching his neck to see around some pine trees. It was a dark colored, large station wagon looking vehicle, but

Izrael didn't recognize it either. They trotted the horses a little quicker until they reached the barn. Poppa nodded to Iz as if to direct him to get the horses put up and jumped off his horse then hurried toward the house.

Izrael began untacking the horses and putting up their saddles and blankets, whistling and talking to Mindee as he put things away. Mindee loved when Iz whistled; she would perk up her ears and trot around, as if she were dancing to his whistling tunes. Izrael felt good. It had been a busy week full of hard work, but it was a good week. He felt closer to Poppa than ever and felt like his future plans were finally becoming reality. How could anything go wrong, he wondered to himself, almost in a prophetic thought? Once he had the horses settled, had fed them, and given them plenty of water, Izrael picked up his and Poppa's bags and started the short walk towards the house. As he got closer, he could hear voices, and they were sounding louder and louder the closer he got.

The next few moments threatened Izrael's happiness, and his plans. As he hurried into the house, the voices he had heard outside grew more intense. Suddenly, his heart sank. He recognized one of the voices. It was Carolina. As he listened over the sound of his own heart beating, he realized the other voice was her mother, Ms. Parker, and she was doing most of the talking. He wondered who she was talking with; was it Momma, or Poppa, or one of his sisters? Izrael's steps quickened and when he stepped onto the porch he heard his sister, Lucy, say, "Izrael is not here right now and we don't know when he will be back!" At that Carolina blurted, "Does he still live here?" She turned towards the door and saw Izrael on the porch and screeched, "There he is! You lied to me; he is here!"

Lucy rushed to the door and stepped out, grabbed Izrael's arm and whispered, "I was trying to get rid of them, Iz." "It's okay, Lucy," Izrael whispered back. "Where's Momma, and what about Poppa?" was Izrael's next quick question to Lucy. Lucy smiled nervously at Izrael and told him Momma had taken some food to the neighbor who was sick and had children to feed so Momma had doubled up their dinner in order to share with their neighbor. "That sounds like Momma," Iz thought and then quickly turned his attention back to their visitors. "Where's Poppa?" were Izrael's next words to Lucy and as he turned towards the kitchen where the voices were coming from, he ran straight into Poppa's chest. Iz looked directly at Poppa who had a very serious look on his face. Izrael knew what that meant; Poppa was not happy.

When Izrael entered the kitchen, he made eye contact first with Ms. Parker, and then Carolina. "Good afternoon, ma'am" was all Izrael could say. Ms. Parker glared hard at Izrael but did not say a word. It was Carolina who started talking immediately. "Oh, Izrael, I have missed you so much, you have no idea! I have so much to tell you and Momma was hoping to talk with your momma, can we wait for her to get back?" Carolina finally stopped to take a breath. "I – I – I'm not sure. We weren't expecting you," Izrael shot back at Carolina. This time, when he looked at Carolina he realized she looked thinner. Her bulging stomach was no longer bulging. This made Izrael feel sick to his stomach, and he was very nervous.

Momma walked through the door at that moment, and the rest became almost a blur to Izrael. Over the next couple of hours, he often stopped to check himself with a pinch to his arm, wondering if he was in a bad dream? It wasn't a dream. His worst nightmares had come true.

Ms. Parker made Carolina tell Izrael and his parents, and sisters why they had come. Carolina started out talking about how she and Izrael had met on her first day at Forrest Lane High School and what a gentleman he had been towards her always. This made Izrael suspicious; the last time he saw her she had made a lot of accusations that were not true. Where was she going with this now?

"Everything was very good, very innocent and kind, until..." Carolina paused, took a deep breath, pushed tears out, and finished her statement, "....until that one awful afternoon." "What afternoon??!" Izrael interrupted loudly and with a crack in his voice. Poppa shot Iz a harsh look. Carolina looked up angrily at Izrael who had been standing across the table from Carolina since he entered the kitchen. Carolina sobbed loudly, grabbed her hankie and blew her nose so hard and loud, Momma jumped.

As Carolina described the events of the afternoon she was referring to, Izrael could hardly believe what he was hearing. None of it was true. None of it. Carolina went on, describing being alone during her walk home when suddenly she heard running feet. She wasn't sure where it was coming from and turned quickly to find Izrael chasing after her. She felt a surge of fear and stopped, yelled out to Izrael, and waited for him to catch up. Izrael was out of breath, as if he had been running from something, or someone. Carolina asked him what was wrong. Izrael didn't answer her. He simply grabbed her by her arm and pulled her to the side of the road, then into the bushes and underneath several tall pines. At this point Carolina described herself screaming at Izrael to tell her what was wrong and asking what he was doing. Carolina described Izrael's eyes looking wild and out of control. What happened next was left to the imagination, as Carolina only said these words, "He stole my innocence that afternoon."

Izrael turned all of his attention to Momma and Poppa. Momma had tears streaming down her face and Iz could not manage to look in her eyes. Poppa's face was red with fury. Izrael felt weakness fill his whole body, as if he could melt right there in front of his parents. Poppa spoke next and said calmly but firmly, "Izrael, your guests are still here. We will discuss this further this evening." With that, Izrael turned back to Carolina and shouted, "YOU'RE A LIAR! YOU KNOW I NEVER DID ANY OF THAT! YOU ARE JUST LIKE YOUR MOMMA; ALL THOSE RUMORS MUST BE TRUE!" Carolina's jaw dropped, "What are you talking about, Izrael?" "Oh, I've heard the rumors about your momma and you having to leave California after stealing money from your grandfather….!" At that Ms. Parker stood quickly to her feet but before she could speak, Poppa interrupted Izrael sternly, "Let's all try to settle down a minute. We do not have to yell. Let's catch our breath before we say anything more."

Izrael stood silent for several seconds then looked directly at Carolina and calmly asked, "Why are you doing this? You know I would never do anything like this to you. Why are you making up such lies about me? What did I do to deserve this?" "What did you do?" Carolina said in her loud shrilling voice! "You rejected me and then you RAPED ME!!"

With those words screeching in the air, Izrael fell hard to his knees. His hands were shaking and soon his whole body was shaking, he scrambled to his feet and turned to Momma who was still crying. Izrael took Momma's hands and through sobs begged her, "Please believe me, Momma, I didn't do this. I would never do anything like this, Momma, you know me better than anyone. How could I ever hurt someone in this way?" Momma tried to speak but words would not come through the tears and the hurt she was feeling. Izrael had broken her heart and he could barely stand it. The anger and the fury towards Carolina were boiling inside him but he knew he had to contain it, for now. Poppa didn't say a word. Izrael's sisters had been in the next room listening quietly. He could hear their sniffling. "How could this be happening?" Izrael wondered out loud. He did not realize he had said it out loud until Ms. Parker spoke up. Her cruel words rang out like a dragon's fire throughout the house, "I'm too much of a proper lady to say how this happened, young man!"

Suddenly Momma turned to Ms. Parker and with a calm tone asked her and Carolina to kindly leave their home. Izrael could hardly believe it; even Poppa looked surprised. "Leave?" Ms. Parker shrieked, "Aren't you going to ask about the baby??"

CHAPTER 32

"THE REAL TRUTH"

"A baby?" was all Poppa could muster after the events of the day. He and Momma had settled into their comfortable chairs to talk after dinner. They sat in silence, from what Izrael could gather. No words. Just what Poppa had said as he sat down in the chair. It seemed like hours had passed before Izrael finally heard their voices speaking in quiet tones. Most days he would have been curious what they spoke of, but tonight he stayed in his room and prayed, and wrote in his journal. Most of what he wrote were questions. He could hardly believe what had taken place. How could he have become friends with such a girl as Carolina, he wondered to himself. And what happened to her baby? No one answered Ms. Parker's question. It was as though everyone was afraid to ask. There would be another time, Izrael was certain, when he would find out more about the baby. Izrael could not help but wonder whose baby Carolina had given birth to. She accused him, but he had never been with any girl in that way and had no plans to do so in the near future. He had always planned to wait until he was married. He and Poppa had talked about girls and how dangerous it was to have any kind of serious relationship with a girl until he was ready to be married. Izrael had agreed with Poppa and even more so after hearing what had happened to Grandpa K and the woman who claimed she was his daughter.

At that moment Izrael realized history was repeating itself! He bolted from his bed where he had been laying and dashed into the family room where Momma and Poppa were still seated. He forgot his manners and blurted out, "It's just like what happened to Grandpa K, Poppa, remember?!" Poppa had been seated with his hands over his face and looked up startled. Izrael repeated himself faster and faster until Poppa stood to his feet. The silence was deafening. Finally, Poppa looked Izrael directly in his eyes and asked, "Are you sure, Iz?"

"Yes, Poppa, yes, I promise you, I never touched Carolina in any inappropriate way. I would never do that. We talked about girls and I have never forgotten what you told me, how to treat girls, Poppa. Please, believe me!"

"I do believe you, Iz. Momma and I have been talking and we believe you, son." At these words Izrael fell into Poppa's arms and sobbed. The three stood in the family room huddled close without speaking. This was a moment in time Izrael would never forget.

What was to come would change their lives forever, but what mattered most was their family bond could not be shaken. The trust and the safety of family is what kept Izrael from falling apart, and he felt closer to his parents than ever before.

Izrael stepped out of the room, towards the kitchen and heard his sisters talking. He followed their voices and found them sitting together in Lucy and Cilla's room. They all ran to him when he entered as he felt their arms wrap around him altogether. No words were needed. This moment made Izrael feel stronger. He knew he could handle whatever Carolina and Ms. Parker had planned. He had the support of his family and nothing, or no one, would ever hurt them. The Kammer family was solid. The Parker family did not know what was ahead for them.

CHAPTER 33

"LIFE CHANGES"

It was a couple of weeks before Carolina and her mother attempted to contact the Kammer family again. This time their contact came by mail. It was a letter, written by Ms. Parker, addressed to Suzanah.

Suzanah had picked up the mail the morning it arrived but had waited for Iz and Alex K to return from working to open it. They sat together at the kitchen table, knowing that whatever was in the letter, it would not be pleasant. Suzanah asked Alex K to open it. Slowly, he opened the envelope, using his pocketknife to carefully slide across the top of the envelope, to be sure nothing tore. As he unfolded the letter, Izrael's heart raced. He was anxious to know what lies were written in black and white about him. When Alex K opened the letter, it was blank, but a photograph fell onto the table. Alex K picked it up and quickly handed it to Suzanah. She gasped. Izrael leaned towards his momma and saw the top of a baby's head. He squinted and said loudly, "They sent a picture of her baby?"

"Looks like a baby to me," Poppa muttered. "Oh, my goodness," Momma whispered.

Izrael took the photo from Momma, looked closer and turned it over. He read out loud what was scribbled on the back, "To my daddy with love, Jane Mae." Izrael's face was flushed and he could feel sweat building on the back of his neck. Poppa then took the photo from Izrael and again muttered to himself, but loud enough for Iz and Momma to hear him say, "that's an ugly baby!" "Alex K!" Momma reacted quickly. "Well, it's true, look at her!" Poppa answered. Iz had thought the same thing to himself. The baby was not a pretty baby. She had a lot of dark hair that stood straight up. Her eyes were almost sunken looking and very far apart, her face was wide with a wide nose in the middle. She wasn't smiling in the picture and her ears stuck out further than her hair on the sides of her large head. "Poor little baby," Momma finally said, "She is definitely not a Kammer baby!" Izrael looked again. Momma was right. All of their baby pictures were cute. Izrael almost laughed but the mood was not light. In fact, it was very somber.

Izrael began to feel a sadness for Carolina. They had been friends, after all. He almost felt sorry for her. How desperate could she be, to make up lies about him in order to cover the truth of what happened to her? For the first time, Izrael began to wonder what really did happen. He was not sure if he would ever know. Maybe he should try to contact her, or find someone he trusted to talk with her? Who would that be? Izrael's next thought was of his buddies; maybe MJ would help him. What would MJ think of all this? Izrael suddenly had a flashback to the day he had spent with his buddies picking up supplies. He remembered MJ talking to a girl and Iz had barely seen the back of a car driving away. Was it Carolina's car? MJ had shrugged her off quickly, almost seeming secretive about the girl in the car. What was that about? The sadness began to overwhelm Izrael to the point that Momma noticed. "Let me get you something to eat, Iz, you look pale," she said as she stood from the table. "I'm really not hungry, Momma, but thank you," he answered without looking up.

Poppa then stood up and looking right at Izrael stated, "Let's get back to work, Iz. This ranch won't take care of itself." Izrael jumped up and followed Poppa, as they would attempt to get their minds back on the work they needed to take care of that afternoon.

The two could be seen from the house. Momma often stepped out on the back porch and sat in her favorite spot to watch Alex K and Izrael working the land. She had always been so proud of her husband and son. Today was no different. Yes, they had new challenges to face, but she still felt pride as she watched from a distance that day.

Suzanah Grace began to pray. Her heart felt heavy, and she knew the only thing she could do was pray. Phina and Nikola were playing nearby and heard their momma's voice. They knew where to find her. Suzanah usually sang while she prayed, and the girls always loved hearing her sing. They sat down on the porch to listen. This time they noticed she sounded sad in her voice. Phina moved next to Suzanah and laid her head on her lap, then sang quietly with her. Suzanah looked down and began to stroke Phina's hair. As Suzanah prayed, she began to feel how blessed she was to have 4 beautiful daughters and a handsome son. She knew that appearances were not everything and that her children were all precious on the inside as well. Knowing that pride was not necessarily what God wanted her to feel, she prayed for each child by name, as she did every day. Suzanah prayed for God's protection and wisdom over each of them, ending her prayer with thanks for all the blessings in their lives. Suzanah also prayed for baby Jane Mae, as she felt concern for the child's future.

Nikola became restless and began to stir. Suzanah opened her eyes and reached her arms out to Nikola to come to her. Nikola quickly settled into her momma's lap, giving her a soft kiss on the cheek. "Thank you, my darling," said Suzanah as she softly kissed Nikola back.

With difficult times likely ahead, the family still had so much to be thankful for. Suzanah thanked God for all He provided and hugged Nikola one more time before standing to get back in the house for her afternoon chores and begin the preparations for dinner.

Lucy and Cilla had already begun the process. Suzanah looked at each of them as she stepped into the kitchen and reached her arms out towards the two of them. Both girls rushed over and hugged their momma tightly, reassuring her of their love for her and the whole family. "We are so blessed, girls, aren't we?" Suzanah whispered. "Yes, Momma, yes we are," both girls gushed. "We will get through this, Momma," Lucy added, smiling through soft tears.

Hard times were no stranger to the Kammer family. However, because of their faith in God, each of them knew not to fear and to trust in God and His ultimate plan.

CHAPTER 34

"MOMMA'S TURN"

The next several days were more of the same issues and conversations among the family. Izrael spent more time with Mindee and even had a few opportunities to run, into the canyon. His second favorite thing to do still, after riding Mindee, was to run. It was his escape from any worries or problems he might be having. It had been a while since he had run and Izrael could feel it. He knew this time his mind was trying to run from Carolina and her lies. Suzanah knew it too. She could always tell when Iz was running for a reason. She resisted asking him about it, but truly did not need to ask. Carolina's lies were wearing him out. Suzanah had been praying for answers ever since Ms. Parker and Carolina had shown up at their house. Over the past few days, she had begun feeling a need to talk with Carolina's mother. Suzanah talked with Alex K, asking his opinion. While he felt some resistance, Alex K knew Suzanah needed to get this done. He gave his blessing and insisted he would drive her to Ms. Parker's home. Suzanah agreed and made the arrangements to go the next day. Alex K did not trust Ms. Parker. She was much larger than Suzanah and Alex K knew if anything got out of hand, Ms.

Parker could hurt Suzanah, physically, but he hoped it would not come to that. Alex K shook off these thoughts, as he knew his thoughts were his worst enemy and he did not need to let it get to that point.

The next morning Suzanah talked with Izrael after breakfast. She was very careful to explain to Iz how she had not changed her belief in what he had told them about his relationship with Carolina. She also stated she was not sure what exactly she would be saying to Carolina and her mother; she just knew she needed to go see them. While Izrael understood everything Momma said, he was still a little nervous about the whole idea. He had offered to go with her, but Momma felt this needed to be woman-to-woman. Izrael silently took a big sigh of relief, as he was not feeling up to seeing Carolina, nor her mother. In fact, he would be happy to never see either of them again. The thought of the two of them, and the baby, made him sick to his stomach.

The drive across the valley and into another canyon was always beautiful and relaxing. Today was a little different, as Suzanah and Alex K both felt anxiety about this trip. Suzanah spent the drive praying, even while she looked out at the beautiful scene around them. She asked God to guide her words, to keep her calm and that all would be in His will, however things turned out. She was a little nervous to see the baby for the first time too. Suzanah wasn't sure what made her nervous about the baby, but something just did not feel right. She would know soon enough.

When they came to the last hill, Alex K's truck sputtered to reach the top of the steep and rocky road. As they cleared the top, they could see a house sitting out alone to the left across a grassy field. Suzanah felt her stomach flip over. She wasn't sure if it was nerves or the pickup hopping over the top of the steep incline. Soon Alex K was turning onto the long drive, in front of the house. There were few trees, so it was easy to see the house. Suzanah remembered the house. One of her friends from high school, MaryLou, lived there with her family. She thought the family still owned it. She had heard that MaryLou's parents had passed away and that MaryLou rented it out to Ms. Parker. Suzanah wondered if MaryLou had ever met the Parker family, and if she had would she still have rented it to them? Suzanah quickly asked God's forgiveness for her judgment and turned her attention back to why she was here in the first place.

Alex K pulled up to the side of house, under a shade tree and told Suzanah he would wait there for her. He also reminded Suzanah what to do if she got uncomfortable at any point. She was to step out onto the porch and drop her hat by accident. Alex K would be there in two seconds. He could clearly see the porch from where he parked. Suzanah promised Alex K, kissed his cheek, and climbed out of the pickup. While Suzanah walked up the front steps she could hear the baby crying which made her uncomfortable. The crying was followed by a sharp screeching voice, "Shut that baby up right now!" Suzanah guessed it was Ms. Parker and her guess proved right when Carolina's voice followed, "I'm sorry, Momma! I don't know why she won't stop crying!" Suzanah stood on the porch for several seconds before knocking. She considered dropping her hat but decided she had come all this way and did not want it to be for nothing, so she knocked. No response. Suzanah knocked again, this time harder. Finally, Ms. Parker stepped onto the porch forcefully, almost hitting Suzanah with the door. Ms. Parker flatly said, "Well, don't just stand there, come inside!" Again, Suzanah felt hesitant, but she pushed through her anxiety and stepped inside.

The house was a mess. Suzanah had never seen anything like it. There were shoes, socks and toys all over the floor. Dirty plates were on the kitchen table, as if left in the middle of a meal never to be touched again. Suzanah imagined rats crawling everywhere among the various options of leftovers. The thought made Suzanah nauseous. "Come have a seat, Mrs. Kammer, over here." Ms. Parker said, again, flatly. Suzanah stepped into the sitting room and sat in a chair across from Ms. Parker. Carolina and the baby were not in the room, but the baby was still crying. Ms. Parker yelled to Carolina, "What are you doing in there, Carolina? Why is that baby still crying?" "I'm sorry, Momma, I'm coming," Carolina yelled from the other room.

Within a few moments, Carolina and the baby stepped into the room. Suzanah remembered the day they had received a picture of Jane Mae Parker and how the family had reacted. She looked away for a minute, swallowed back tears and said hello to Carolina. Carolina greeted Suzanah politely and sat down next to Ms. Parker with the baby in her lap. "So, this is Jane Mae?" Suzanah asked, her voice almost cracking. "Yes, and she's not a very good baby," Ms. Parker said gruffly. "Momma!" Carolina whined at Ms. Parker who ignored Carolina and asked Suzanah why she had come.

Suzanah took a deep breath, said a soft prayer for guidance, and began. "Ever since we received the picture of little Jane Mae," Suzanah began, "I haven't stopped thinking about her. I wanted to see if she was okay, if all of you were okay and if there was anything you needed. Can we help with meals, or babysitting? I have four daughters who are very good with children."

Ms. Parker interrupted bluntly, "Babysitting?? That's what you are offering? Where's Jane Mae's daddy? Why didn't he come with you? I think we have a wedding to plan, not scheduling babysitting! What's WRONG with you Mrs. Kammer?? These two kids need to start planning for their baby's future."

Suzanah was not sure what to say next. She started to get up but chose not to. Rather, she gently said, "Ms. Parker, I believe there has been a misunderstanding of what happened between our children. I believe my son when he said he did not touch Carolina in an inappropriate way, and I wanted to offer my help to you both." At that, Ms. Parker stood; her height appearing to be even taller than her real height which was much taller than Suzanah. She held her head high, her breasts pushed forward and her hands grasping her hips. She quite loudly cleared her throat in a deep growl like a bear, and began, "Mrs. Kammer, you are wrong. You have no idea what you are talking about. What your son did is despicable and cruel. Now, what are YOU going to do about this?"

Suzanah was stunned. At first, she didn't know how to react. This woman, and her daughter, were accusing her only son of lying. That didn't settle well with Suzanah. Finally, she stood, picked up her jacket that had been lying next to her on the torn couch, turned quickly and headed to the front door. "You're leaving?" growled Ms. Parker, "we haven't finished yet. There is much more to discuss!" Suzanah turned to look Ms. Parker directly in the eyes and said flatly, "For now, we are finished, Ms. Parker. Don't call me, I will call you!"

Suzanah rushed through the door, down the steep stairs off the porch and hurried to the pickup where Alex K now stood outside of, on the drivers' side. He immediately could see that Suzanah was upset so he ran around the truck to open the passenger door and assist her in climbing onto the seat. Suzanah's heart was racing, and she was breathing fast and loud. Alex K knew not to ask yet. He would give her time to catch her breath, say a silent prayer, and let her do the talking.

CHAPTER 35

"MAKING PLANS"

During the ride home, Suzanah did give herself time to catch her breath. She prayed, as usual, for God to be her guide even as she spoke about Ms. Parker and Carolina. She knew, in her heart, that if she had ill thoughts, it would be sinful in God's eyes, so she took the time to talk with God before she shared with Alex K.

After about 30 minutes, Alex K interrupted Suzanah's thoughts and asked if she was okay. Suzanah opened her eyes and turned toward her husband. She had always seen the goodness and gentleness in Alex K that most others did not see. When he looked at her the way he did now, Suzanah felt loved and cared for. She gave him a quick, small smile and said, "It was awful, Alex. I have never met anyone like Ms. Parker, bless her heart." "Bless her heart?" Alex K blurted back but stopped when he saw the seriousness of Suzanah's expression. She continued, "Ms. Parker and Carolina insist that our son did this horrible thing to Carolina. They would not listen to anything I tried to say and the only subject they wanted to discuss was wedding planning! Can you believe that Alex? I have never been so insulted in all my life and I do not want our son married to that awful young lady!" "I don't either, Suzanah, I don't either," Alex K answered as he reached over and squeezed her hand.

Over the remainder of the drive home Suzanah described what took place during the visit and the two talked about strategies. They agreed to talk with Izrael later that evening. Both Alex K and Suzanah knew it was not going to be an easy fight with the Parker family, and the Parker's had no idea what they were up against. The Kammer family was known for being strong and sticking together. Other families in the valley admired them and some were jealous of their strength as a family. Carolina Parker and her momma were no match for the Kammer's. Suzanah suspected that part of the reason Ms. Parker acted the way she did was out of intimidation. She also realized that could be of benefit to Izrael.

Momma was exhausted when she and Poppa arrived back home. Izrael was finishing up work and his 4 sisters were preparing dinner so Momma would not have to. Momma was very pleased when she stepped into the aromas coming from the kitchen. "Oh, I have the very best girls in the valley!" Momma exclaimed as she hung her jacket and put up her things. After she had washed up, she joined her daughters in the kitchen, hugging each girl and giving them a soft kiss on the cheek. Nikola wiped her hands down the front of her apron, turned to Momma and hugged her so tight Momma gasped for air, exaggerating to get a giggle out of her sweet youngest daughter. "Thank you, Nik, you are so sweet," Momma responded. She jumped right into the dinner prep which was nearly finished. The family was together at the table within minutes after Momma and Poppa arrived.

"Making Plans"

    The conversation at the table was simple, mostly about the weather and some of the smaller animals around the farm. Nikola and Josephina were giggling about the pigs and the noises they made when the girls fed them earlier. Poppa finally snapped at the girls, indicating it was not proper conversation at the dinner table. "Yes, sir, Poppa, we're sorry," the girls answered in unison which only made them giggle again. The whole family laughed together after them, then began clearing the table. Izrael carried his plate to the sink near Momma and whispered, "Are you okay, Momma? How was the visit?" "Stay close, son, Poppa and I want to talk with you as soon as we finish clean up," Momma answered. "Yes, Momma, I will stay and help," was Izrael's quick answer.

    One by one the family dispersed from the kitchen to their bedrooms, or the family room. Only Momma and Izrael were left in the kitchen, then Poppa returned. "Sit down, Iz," Poppa instructed. Izrael sat down immediately, followed by both of his parents on each side of him. "This looks serious," Iz said softly. "It truly is serious, Izrael Shane," Poppa said in his tone that meant Iz better be listening. Momma had hung up her apron and closed the door between the kitchen and the family room, to avoid the girls hearing their conversation. This made Izrael even more nervous. Poppa looked angry and Momma looked worried.

    Momma started talking, "Izrael Shane, things are not good with Carolina and her momma. They are insisting the child is yours and they are not open to a conversation about it nor trying to find out the truth of what happened. Now we need a plan…." Izrael's face interrupted Momma. He was flushed and Momma knew that look. She knew he was about to cry. Izrael's eyes welled up and his chin quivered. The tears rolled and he hung his head low over the table, nearly touching his forehead on the table linen in front of him. "Izrael, what is it?" Momma said in an anxious tone. "I can't believe this is happening to me, Momma, to all of the family. I didn't do this. I would never do such a thing, Momma, never. All I did was be Carolina's friend and spend time with her when others didn't like her. I liked her and I even started to enjoy the sound of her laugh. We had fun, but we never did anything together like she says we did. Why is she saying this, why?" At that, Izrael, crossed his hands in front of him on the table, dropped his head and sobbed. "Oh, Alex, what are we going to do?" Momma breathed out as she rubbed Izrael's arm nearest to her. Poppa had not said a word yet, with all the emotion happening he waited which was just like Poppa to wait.

Poppa leaned over Izrael and hugged his shoulders, as he leaned into him. His right hand caressed the top of Izrael's head and Iz could feel Poppa's breath. It surprised him to feel Poppa like this. As he slowly began to raise up, Poppa leaned back and sat back down in his chair. Izrael felt the strength of Poppa flowing through him. He felt warm and he felt encouraged. He realized at that moment that he had his father's strength and that emotions were temporary. After all, he was a Kammer. Izrael pushed his chair back, wiped his eyes, crossed his arms, looked at both of his parents and boldly said, "Okay, I am ready. What's next?"

The three huddled together for the next couple of hours, going over strategy to break down the lies. By the time they finished for the night, all the girls had gone to bed. Momma got up quickly to go check her daughters while Iz and Poppa moved into the family room. Izrael was exhausted. He could feel how the stress had gotten to him. His anxiety had shown up earlier, and Poppa showed him how to handle it. At this moment, he was sure they could deal with anything. As long as he had Momma and Poppa, Izrael knew everything would be alright.

Poppa was settling back in his chair. He reached over to pick up the magazine he had been reading, leaned back, and shut out the rest of reality. Izrael sat at the game table. The girls had started working on a puzzle a few days before. Iz filled in a few pieces then got up to begin his bedtime routine. He was asleep almost before his head hit the pillow. Izrael often worried about sleep before falling asleep, as his dreams were vivid and seemed so real. These days he dreamed of a crying baby. He would wake up in the middle of the night nearly wanting to get up and go find the baby but realized it was a dream and would go back to sleep. Tonight, the exhaustion took over and Izrael slept through the night. It was the rest he had been needing for so long.

CHAPTER 36

"NEXT STEPS"

Morning came soon and the Kammer men were hard at work. The distraction of work was just what Izrael needed. Momma and the girls were busy with chores. It seemed to be a normal day again. A "normal day" is truly what everyone needed. Even the younger girls had felt the pressures of all the anxiety in the family. Izrael was working on a fence post near the goats' pen. Nikola had slipped out of the house and was playing nearby. One of her favorite games was to have a stare-down with the male goat from outside of his pen. The goat seemed to love it too because he was always ready when he heard Nikola's voice. He would kick at the dirt with his front right hoof until she came over. Then the two would stare at each other until one kicked the dirt; then the male goat would charge at the fence and Nikola would scream and run around in circles giggling the whole time. The whole event was humorous to watch.

When Iz heard Nikola's voice, he expected to find her teasing the male goat. Instead, she was sitting on a stump and didn't seem to be doing anything. "Hey, Nik, what's going on?" Izrael shouted towards Nikola. Nikola did not respond so Iz said it again. This time Nikola looked up surprised to see Izrael at the other side of the pen. "Nothing!" she yelled back. Izrael set down his tools and walked around to where Nikola was sitting and sat down next to her. "Are you okay, Nik?" Nikola shrugged her shoulders as if to say, "I don't know." "Come on, sis, you can talk to your big brother, that's what I'm here for," Iz answered. After some hesitation Nikola finally asked, "Iz, are you going to have a baby?" Izrael was so surprised by the question he almost laughed but knew better and instead put his arm around Nikola, pulled her close and said, "No, I'm not, Nikola. There are some bad things being said by some people but none of it is true. If anyone asks you, tell them to come ask me. It's not anyone's business but our family and I promise you, we are taking care of it. You do not need to worry your pretty little head about me, you hear me, Nik?" Nikola snuggled her head against Izrael's chest and whispered, "I love you, big brother!" "I love you too, Nik, I will always be here for you," answered Izrael.

Nikola bolted up and went straight to her game with the male goat. Izrael laughed this time out loud and said, "You get him, Nik!" Nikola giggled and the game continued.

Izrael loved his sisters so much. His goal was to always protect all of them and be the best brother he could possibly ever be, for each one of them. They all loved him too. He always felt he was the luckiest guy in the valley for having the best sisters ever. While most of his friends complained about their siblings, Izrael never did. He would just smile and listen to them, always feeling thankful for his sisters.

The following days were much of the same routine for Izrael and his family. Things seemed to be settling down and

"Next Steps"

no one had heard from Carolina or Ms. Parker, until another letter came in the mail.

This time the letter was addressed to Izrael. The envelope was written in messy handwriting, *"Mr. Izrael Shane Kammer"* and across the bottom was the word, *"CONFIDENTIAL"* in all capital letters. The letter was on the kitchen table when Izrael and Poppa returned from working. "What's this?" Poppa asked. "I'm not sure, it's addressed to Iz. Come, open it, son," Momma gently urged Izrael. "We have a little time before dinner is ready. Let's see what it is," Momma continued. Izrael pulled a chair back from the table and slipped open the envelope that had loosened its seal during the delivery, making it easy to open. Inside the envelope were two pieces of paper; the first was a note with only one sentence, "Here is your proof." The other paper was folded neatly. As Izrael began to unfold it, Momma gasped. She recognized what kind of document it was but did not say a word. Izrael's eyes opened wide as he read the words on the birth certificate for baby Jane Mae. Her last name was noted as "Kammer," he couldn't believe it. "Momma, Poppa! Look at this, now their lies are in black and white!" Izrael dropped the papers on the table and leaned back in his chair. Poppa picked it up and started turning red. Momma looked at it next then set it back on the table without saying anything.

The war continued. It was time for a family huddle. Time to put all the cards on the table and make sure everyone was aware of all the lies and get down to the truth.

CHAPTER 37

"FAMILY MEETING"

After dinner Momma told the family she had a surprise for everyone. She turned to the stove and picked up a fresh baked cherry pie, Izrael's favorite, and all the family loved her cherry pie. "What's the occasion?" piped Josephina. "It's not anyone's birthday," added Nikola. The older girls pulled out the dessert plates and forks and everyone perked up. "No birthday necessary," Momma said, "I just thought the family needed a little pick-me-up. We've had a few hard weeks lately. Now let's enjoy this pie!" "Yes, let's dig in," Poppa said only with a little more serious tone. Izrael smiled at Momma, knowing she was doing her best to keep the family close and as happy as possible, even in the midst of a stressful time. Iz knew he had the best momma in the valley, and he was very thankful.

Once everyone had finished dessert, and the dishes were picked up, Poppa started talking. "We want the whole family to understand what is happening with Izrael's friend, Carolina. As you know, she and her mother have been communicating with Izrael, Momma and I recently. You may not know everything that has been going on, so we wanted to explain it because at times like this, family support is very important."

"Are we talking about Izrael being a daddy, Poppa?" asked Nikola in her innocent childlike voice. "Oh, honey, we do want to talk about what has been happening with Izrael, but he is not a daddy," Momma soothed Nikola as she stroked the back of her hair. "Let's let Poppa talk for now. You can ask questions when he is done," Momma added. "Okay, Momma," Nikola said as she snuggled into Momma's side and wrapped her arms around Momma's left arm. Poppa smiled gently at his youngest child. The girls all had special places in Poppa's heart. He loved them dearly and planned to always protect each of them. No boy would ever hurt his girls the way some boy had hurt Carolina. The thought made him shudder. Poppa cleared his throat and began, "Yes, girls, we want all of you to understand everything. Izrael has been blamed for something he had nothing to do with. We don't know the truth because Carolina and Ms. Parker are hiding the truth from us. We don't really know why they are doing this, but what they are doing to Iz, to our family, is not good." Poppa looked across the table at Izrael who had been looking down at the table while Poppa spoke. "Izrael Shane, lift up your chin, son! Do not lower your head in shame for something you had nothing to do with, do you understand me?" said Poppa sternly. "Yes, sir, I understand," Iz answered as he sat up straight in his chair and looked over at Nikola who had such a tender and loving look on her face. "I love you, Nik," Iz whispered which made Nikola giggle softly.

"As a family, we need to stand together. Izrael has done nothing wrong. In other words, we are going to discover what the truth is once and for all." Again, Poppa cleared his throat. This time Lucy spoke up, "How can we help, Poppa?" "Yes, tell us what we can do, Poppa" added Priscilla. "We want you girls to talk with your friends, ask them questions in order to find

"Family Meeting"

out who might know something," Poppa responded quickly. "Yes, we can do that," Lucy answered as she looked to Cilla for agreement and who was already nodding in assurance. Cilla added that one of her best friends, Stella, had been talking about Carolina recently. Her younger brother had mentioned Carolina to her and told her he thought Carolina was too pushy. Stella tried to ask more but her brother changed the subject. Cilla looked at Izrael and asked, "Has MJ said anything to you about Carolina?" Iz was a bit surprised by Cilla's question and said he had not talked to MJ since the day he went to town with his buddies for supplies.

As the family continued to discuss various friends who might have information, or know how to go about getting information, Izrael's thoughts went back to the day with his buddies. He remembered MJ having been somewhat secretly talking with a girl in the parking lot when Iz finished paying for his items. Izrael had teased MJ about him having a girlfriend. Iz remembered how MJ had acted strange when he told Izrael she was not anyone he knew and brushed it off rather abruptly. "MJ might know something!" Izrael blurted out. "Why do you think so?" Momma asked. Izrael told his family what he had seen, and everyone agreed it would be a good idea to talk with MJ. "Why don't you invite him for dinner tomorrow, Iz?" Momma suggested. Izrael nodded quickly and the family continued discussing various ideas and friends who might be able to help.

It was a good evening. While the subject was difficult, the Kammer family had stuck with each other and there was nothing more meaningful to Izrael than how his family was supporting him and believing in him.

CHAPTER 38

"MJ"

Izrael and Alex K started work early the following day. They had eaten a small breakfast before leaving the house and had decided to break for lunch a little earlier than usual. "Poppa, do you mind if I ride Mindee over the hill to see MJ and invite him to dinner before I get back to work?" Izrael asked as they were finishing lunch. "Yes, good idea, Iz, you go right ahead," said Poppa. Izrael hurried out to tack up Mindee and head over the hill to look for MJ.

Izrael found MJ working on a broken gate at the entrance of his family's property. "MJ! Hi, MJ!" Iz said loudly as he galloped towards him. "Well, if it isn't Speedy Iz! What are you doing here?" MJ hollered back. As Izrael approached, he was talking and laughing with MJ as they usually did when they greeted each other. Izrael reached down to help MJ hold onto the post as he wrapped wire to hold it all in place. "Thanks, Iz! You got here at just the right moment," MJ loudly blurted out as he worked to finish wrapping the post. "Looks like it, buddy, sure looks like it," Izrael answered. MJ turned to pick up his tools and load up his toolbox. Izrael was about to invite MJ when they heard honking. They turned to see Cliff and Benji pulling up in Cliff's old pickup. "Oh, great," Iz thought to himself. He was about to invite MJ for dinner and the other half of the 4 musketeers showed up.

"What's new?" Benji yelled out from the passenger seat. "What are you doing here, Speedy Iz? Don't you have work to do with your poppa?" The two climbed out of the pickup and walked over to the gate where MJ and Iz were still standing. "Oh, nothing really, just catching up I guess," Izrael muttered. "You okay?" Cliff asked as he popped Iz on the arm in a friendly, buddy kind of pop. "I'm fine," Izrael brushed off Cliff's answer. "You don't seem fine," Cliff muttered back, in an irritated tone. "Did you come over just to harass Iz, guys? Geez, lay off," MJ said in defense of Izrael. "Sorry!" Benji threw in, "Hey we were just stopping by quickly. We have a lot of errands to run for our folks. We saw you two hanging here; didn't mean to offend anyone."

"It's okay!" Izrael jumped in quickly. "I'm just a little tired and trying to keep up with everything lately so I was a little testy back to you guys," he added. "It's all good, but hey, I was wondering something the other day, guys, about the day we all went to town for supplies." "That was a great day, wasn't it?" Cliff chimed in. "Yes, it was, but when I stepped out of the store, all 3 of you were standing by a car that was driving away by the time I caught up to you. I saw the back end of the car, but it didn't occur to me then; was Carolina in that car? Was it her car and was she alone?"

"What, Iz, who?" Cliff stammered while Benji hurried back to Cliff's truck. It was MJ who answered after what seemed like several minutes, "No, Speedy Iz, I told you that day, it was a longtime family friend who I hadn't seen in a while." "Okay, MJ, sorry, I kept thinking about how that car looked like Carolina's from the back." "Well, you can forget about it now, Iz, and you two get on outa here!" MJ hollered as Cliff ran to catch up with Benji who was waiting nervously. Izrael watched as they drove down the road, leaving a thin film of dust in their path. "That dust may never settle," Iz thought to himself.

"Those guys will never grow up, Iz, you know what I mean?" MJ said after they were gone. "Yeah, maybe not," Iz answered turning back towards MJ and remembering why he was there. "Momma wanted me to invite you over for dinner tonight, MJ, what do you say? Can you come over?" "Heck yeah! I never turn down your momma's cookin' Iz! Just let me run inside a minute and make sure my momma doesn't mind; be right back." MJ ran up the short hill and into his home. Izrael climbed onto Mindee's back and walked her down the road a little ways and back while he waited. A few minutes later MJ was back at the gate and let Izrael know he would be there, "What time, Iz?" "Come as soon as you finish up work, MJ. Momma usually has dinner ready around 6:00. She will be so happy to see you, bud!"

At that Izrael tipped his hat and headed back down the road towards home.

MJ arrived a little early for dinner. It was just like MJ to be early. Iz was still cleaning up so when he stepped out of his bedroom, he could hear MJ talking with Momma. Izrael hesitated.

Iz heard Momma's voice going on about how handsome MJ looked and how much she loved the flowers he brought for the table. "Be careful, Momma," Iz said as he walked into the kitchen, "MJ might get an even bigger head with all those compliments!" "Izrael, that's not a nice thing to say," Momma shot back at Iz. "Ha, ha, Iz, that's so funny!" MJ laughed in response. The small talk continued while Momma made the final preparations for dinner, along with Lucy and Priscilla.

Soon the whole family was sitting at the table, passing serving dishes of delicious food around in a sequence, like a dance, waiting for the next move as the dish passed over. The Kammer family never passed serving dishes across the table to someone; they always went around the table in a polite and flowing manner. Once everyone had a full plate, it was time to eat. MJ was the first to compliment Momma. "Everything is delicious, Mrs. Kammer, so very delicious!" MJ exclaimed, trying to be proper and not speak with his mouth full. "Thank you, MJ, the girls and I love to cook, don't we, girls?" "Yes, Momma," the two answered quickly in unison. This made everyone giggle a little and helped to relax the discussion. Poppa began by asking MJ what his future plans entailed. Izrael knew right away that MJ was always good to talk about himself; after all, he was his favorite subject! Iz shook his head to himself and listened intently to everything MJ said. Once dinner was over, the family and MJ all moved to the living room.

"So, how is all your family doing, MJ?" Poppa asked. "Everyone is doing very well, thank you for asking, sir," MJ answered. "That's good to hear," Poppa said quickly then commented about a few projects he and Izrael had been working on recently. "Hard work is a good thing," MJ said but almost in an uneasy tone, as if he were feeling a little uncomfortable suddenly. Iz jumped in and asked MJ if he had seen any of their classmates lately. "Hmm, no not really, Iz, just the usual guys, you know. You've seen them too. Who are you asking about?" MJ asked. "Oh, I don't know, maybe some of the girls from our class. Do you ever talk with any of them anymore now that we are out of high school?" Izrael questioned. "I saw Benji's sister, Tammy, and a few of her friends when I went to town not too long ago, but that's about it, Iz." MJ looked around the room at Izrael's family and realized everyone was listening intently to the conversation. He sat up straight and asked boldly, "Okay, what's really going on here? What's with all the questions and especially all the silence and why is everyone staring at me?"

Lucy unexpectedly piped in and shot out at MJ, "What do you know about Carolina Parker having a baby, MJ?" Poppa turned towards Lucy and sent her a quick but harsh look that made her sit back in her chair and lower her head, as if embarrassed. MJ wasn't quite sure how to respond. Finally, he said, "Carolina Parker had a baby? You know, I had heard that but thought it might be a nasty rumor. I don't really care to know anything about that crazy girl! You know what I mean, right, Iz?" Izrael nodded. "Go on," Momma said gently while smiling at MJ. "There's a lot of talk in the valley right now," MJ began. "People are talking and saying crazy things about that baby. Heck, I even heard she is telling everyone that Izrael is the daddy! Is that true, Iz? Please tell me it's not true!" This time MJ stood to his feet and moved over towards Izrael.

"No, it's NOT true, MJ, and we need your help proving it. Will you help us, please?" "Of course, I'll help, Iz, but I'm not sure what I can do!" MJ answered.

"You can help by asking questions around the valley," Iz started. "You know just about everyone and their dog in this valley, bud!" Everyone laughed briefly, and the two friends began working on ideas of who MJ could talk with about Carolina. Momma and Poppa, almost in unison, leaned back in their chairs and sighed. The girls had all gathered around their puzzle but kept listening.

The next step in their plan to discover the truth was in place. Hope was again teasing the Kammer family, lightly in the air.

CHAPTER 39

"WHOSE BABY IS SHE ANYWAY?"

A few days had passed since MJ had been over to the Kammer's for dinner. He had been hard at work with his own poppa when he had an unexpected visitor show up at his home. As he was putting away tools and cleaning up near the end of the day, MJ heard a loud horn honking. He stepped out of the garage and saw a car coming up the road towards him. MJ stretched his hand across his forehead to block the afternoon setting sun and immediately recognized the car. It was Carolina Parker!

"Oh, great!" MJ stammered to himself. "Just what I need, more drama!" As the car came closer, MJ turned to close the barn door and began walking towards the driver's side. "What do you want?" MJ snapped at Carolina. "Well, what kind of way is that to greet your best friend's future bride?" Carolina gloated right back. "Ha! That will never happen and you're crazy if you think it will!" MJ shot at Carolina and added, "Now, turn around and drive this junk of a vehicle right back down my drive, go on, get lost!" MJ was not about to tolerate Carolina's theatrics. "Why are you so rude to me, MJ? That's not what I remember about you last year, why you were just the opposite, so friendly, and …." "Shut up, Carolina! Now you get out of here, you hear me?!"

MJ turned and nearly ran all the way back towards his house. He was nearly out of breath by the time he was at the front door and yelled, "Momma, I'll be right back. I need to go see Izrael Kammer." "Okay, honey," MJ's momma answered from inside, "but don't be long, dinner will be ready before you know it." "Thanks, Momma, I won't be long."

MJ quickly jumped into his pickup truck and straight to the Kammer ranch. He had to warn Izrael and his family about Carolina and what she was saying.

Iz and Alex K were outside when MJ pulled into their drive. "What's up, MJ?" Izrael hollered towards the pickup. "I need to warn you, Iz, that crazy girl is running around saying she is your bride-to-be, bud! We need a plan and I have an idea."

Alex K shook his head and let the two friends talk. Once they had agreed on MJ's plan, they went into the kitchen to share MJ's idea. "It's a little bit risky, don't you think?" Momma asked, while smiling and adding, "but it just might work!"

Momma began scribbling notes on her notepad while Lucy and Cilla began making a list of names. "This is going to be the biggest, best baby shower ever in this valley," Cilla stated very matter of fact like. "Yes, it is!" Lucy added and the two began to laugh while coming up with various names of young women they knew plus those Izrael had gone to school with and who also knew Carolina. Most of them didn't like Carolina so it would be interesting to see how many of them would come.

MJ headed home and Izrael and Alex K finished out their workday. Izrael managed a few minutes to write in his journal.

"Whose Baby is She Anyway?"

The craziness of the past few days needed to be written down and he didn't want to forget any details just in case any of it came back to haunt him one day. Izrael couldn't help but think of Grandpa K as he wrote. The way their lives intertwined was still perplexing to Iz, but it was also somewhat comforting.

That evening the Kammer women were hard at work making their lists and plans for a baby shower. Poppa wasn't sure how this was going to help but he didn't ask questions. He just stayed quiet and let the planning continue. Izrael felt a little bit like Poppa but also a little hopeful that the truth would soon be revealed.

By the following week, Momma, Lucy, and Priscilla had the invitations ready to mail. Most of the young women in the valley, and their mothers were invited. It would be an outdoor event with lots of delicious food and presents for baby Jane Mae. Iz and Poppa agreed to prepare the area outside, in front of the house, for the party. They cleaned and moved things and even had some help from the younger girls who worked hard to make sure there were no weeds in the yard. Momma was pleased and let them know the yard had never looked prettier. The stage was set. They were ready to host the baby shower the following day.

CHAPTER 40

"SHOWER THEM WITH GIFTS"

It was a warm Sunday afternoon. The weather was perfect for an outdoor event. The slight breeze was just enough to keep everyone cool despite it being late June. The big cherry trees gave plenty of shade and Izrael's sisters had made gallons of tasty lemonade for the occasion. As the guests began arriving, Suzanah began to worry that the guest of honor had not yet arrived. "Don't worry, Momma, Carolina likes to make a big entrance, and I'm sure today will be no exception," Izrael assured her.

Before long, Izrael's prediction had come to pass. The loud obnoxious horn of Carolina's car was echoing through the valley and up their driveway. The horn wasn't the only loud noise, as she approached the sounds of a baby whaling grew louder and louder. "Oh, goodness," Suzanah said, "the baby does not sound happy!" A few ladies gathered nearby giggled quietly and one said rather loudly, "I hear that baby is a handful!"

After Carolina parked, she emerged with a large screaming baby girl. Ms. Parker stepped out of the passenger side of the car and smirked at the guests who were all staring at the baby. "What are you all looking at? Haven't you ever seen a baby girl before?" Ms. Parker snapped. "Not one so ugly," a young daughter of one of the guests answered back rather loudly." "Hush child!" her mother quickly added. A few giggles could be heard but were drowned out by the sounds coming from Jane Mae herself as she screamed and bawled loudly while Carolina bounced her up and down on her hip, trying to quiet her down.

Suzanah took pity on the three and rushed over to urge them towards the patio where the food and presents had been arranged beautifully. Carolina gasped as they stepped closer, "Is this all for Jane Mae?" she asked in a surprised tone. Suzanah stepped in toward Carolina and said, "Well, yes, the ladies in the valley wanted to welcome baby Jane Mae and you and your momma with a baby shower. You are being showered with gifts, young lady." Suzanah thought she saw tears glistening in Carolina's eyes and felt some compassion for her. Those thoughts quickly disappeared when Ms. Parker belted out, "What are you doing here? Trying to bribe us??"

"What? Why would you say that Momma," Carolina squealed at Ms. Parker. "Because I've been around a block or two little lady! These people are trying to buy our trust!" "No, no, Momma, please, let's just sit down and enjoy the party. It looks like a lot of work has gone into preparing. We can at least stay and enjoy everything, please, Momma?" Without answering her daughter, Ms. Parker sat in a chair and reached out to hold baby Jane Mae. Carolina gladly put Jane Mae in her grandmother's lap and looked around for Izrael. She turned towards Suzanah and asked, "Where's Jane Mae's daddy? Is Izrael here?"

"That is a really good question, Carolina, and one all of us here would like to know and maybe we should rephrase the question, 'Who IS Jane Mae's daddy?'" Carolina spun around and saw it was Izrael speaking and everyone else was quiet, so very quiet.

"What are you talking about, my sweet Iz? That is a silly question, everyone knows YOU are her daddy. Who else would it be? Who else could it be?" Carolina was clearly flustered and nervous. Even Ms. Parker sat quietly with baby Jane Mae now asleep in her arms.

Suzanna and Alex K stepped forward towards Carolina and began to explain that the whole valley wanted to help her with needs she would have for her baby and that many gifts had been brought for them. Carolina slowly looked around at everyone. She was surprised by some of the familiar faces of girls from school who obviously had not liked her, but here they were, bringing gifts for her baby. She felt very moved by the generosity and still a little bit suspicious. She turned to Suzanah and asked, "Why are you doing this? It was clear you didn't believe me when I told you that Jane Mae is Izrael's baby. So, what is this all about?"

This time Alex K answered as he turned toward Izrael who was now standing close by his poppa. Alex K began speaking, "The people of this peaceful mountain valley take care of each other. We may not always agree with each other, but we do care. If there is a need, we take turns stepping in to help. Since hearing of your baby there has been a lot of concern, but not caring. We have all agreed that it is time to care. Hence, the party and the presents for baby Jane Mae."

"I, I, I.... I don't know what to say," Carolina quietly responded, followed by a soft sniffle.

Alex K continued, "No one expects you to say or do anything, Carolina, except one thing." "What? I'll do anything you want! This is all so very nice, what can I say or do, Mr. Kammer?"

"Just one thing, Carolina," Alex K stressed again, firmly, while looking at both Carolina and Ms. Parker, "Only one thing. Tell the truth about the father of the baby."

The silence that fell next seemed to fall over the whole valley, and not just in the front yard of the Kammer home. In the distance there were sounds of birds chirping and even the constant tapping of the woodpecker. Woodpeckers were everywhere in the valley. They had their favorite trees. One older gentleman in the valley used to say that woodpeckers never died. They stayed with the same tree and the same family forever, throughout all generations.

At this moment, all the woodpeckers seemed to be tapping in unison, as if they were the drum roll before the announcement; whose baby is Jane Mae? Who is the father?

Carolina began to cry, at first quietly, then in sobs and wails. She eerily sounded like baby Jane Mae when she was crying as they arrived. Her wailing sounds echoed now, almost in unison with the tapping of the woodpeckers. This seemed to last forever. A few people appeared restless and some of the girls who knew Carolina from school were rolling their eyes and whispering with each other. They all appeared to know what Carolina's drama looked like.

Finally, Carolina stopped crying. She turned towards Izrael, then Alex K and Suzanah and said, "I don't know who the father is! I don't know! It was dark, so very dark, and there were two of them there…." Carolina's sobs returned.

Again, a hard silence fell, followed by gasps and ultimately the sound of Ms. Parker as she stood, handing the baby to Suzanah, and stepping to hover over Carolina, "You little liar! How COULD YOU? I want you to get that baby and get in the car right now. You don't deserve any of these gifts here!"

"Shower Them with Gifts"

"Two?!" was all Izrael could say, as he turned towards Suzanah who gave Izrael a look that told him 'Let's talk about this later.'

CHAPTER 41
"ENDINGS AND BROKEN CURSES"

Soon after everyone left, the heavens opened a heavy downpour full of loud thunder and lightning strikes. Poppa always said this kind of rain cleaned away curses. This time it felt appropriate. While Momma and the girls grabbed a few remaining dishes from the front porch table, Poppa and Izrael had hurried off to check the animals. All were accounted for and safe from the storm. As they entered the house, they were greeted by Momma and two warm, dry towels.

Once everyone was dry and comfortable and the party clean-up had been completed, Momma and Poppa were heard talking quietly in their comfortable chairs. The four girls had gathered around the current puzzle and Iz made his way to join Momma and Poppa to talk about the events of the day. He felt exasperated and a bit sad. He couldn't help but feel sorry for Carolina; after all, they had been good friends at one point.

"I feel sorry for her too, Izrael," Momma said empathetically as he stepped into the room. "How did you know what I was thinking, Momma?" Iz answered lightly. "Mommas know everything, son, don't you know that by now?" Poppa joked. "I do know that Poppa, and truthfully, I like it that way," Iz answered this time smiling at Momma. "What a day!" was Momma's next comment, "what a day, indeed! It is truly a shame what Carolina has done to herself and to her baby," Momma added. "Yes, it is," Poppa noted, "but thank the Good Lord we are done with all three of them!"

"I'm not so sure we are, Poppa," Izrael said slowly. "What do you mean, son?" Momma asked, almost sounding as if she already knew the answer. "I want to help them, Momma, is that strange?" Izrael asked. "It's not strange at all, Izrael. In fact, it is quite noble of you to say this," Momma answered immediately. "I have been thinking about how we can help them too, Iz. Poppa and I were just talking about letting them know, again, that we can help with babysitting, and I will take them biscuits and other food when we can." "That is so nice, Momma, I know that will be a great help for them," Izrael answered, "and I can do some chores around their house now and then. I remember how overgrown some of the weeds around the front of their house looked the last time.... Well, I will do what I can for them too, Momma and Poppa, but I can't help but also wonder what happened to her, especially when she said there were two of them!" Poppa nodded in agreement, "I agree, Iz, but I really think we need to leave that alone. Whatever happened to Carolina is none of our business. Families in the valley take care of their own problems like that. We will not push her to tell more, nor will we try to find out who those two boys were. Do you understand, Izrael?" Izrael glanced at Momma who gave him the look indicating she agreed with Poppa. "Yes sir, I understand, and I promise not to ask her any questions," Iz

"Endings and Broken Curses"

said to both his momma and poppa. "Good boy, Iz, good boy," was Poppa's last response to the topic.

"There's something else I want to talk about with you both," Izrael added. "What's that, son, go ahead, we're listening," Poppa replied. "It's the curse, Poppa! It's finally broken! We broke it, all of us working together. What happened to Grandpa K seemed like it was happening to me, but we broke it! I am so very relieved," Izrael breathed a huge sigh of relief and sunk back into his chair. "It's not a broken curse, son,' Momma spoke gently. "What do you mean it's not, Momma?" "The truth broke it son, just like Jesus said in the Bible, the truth shall set you free," Momma answered.

In the meantime, Carolina and her mother, Ms. Parker, had also been talking about what to do next. "Oh, Momma," Carolina whined, "I thought I was going to be Mrs. Izrael Kammer soon, it's just not fair, oh, it's just so awful!" "Quit all that whining, girl, and spend your energy figuring out what to do next," Ms. Parker snapped. "You are still going to need a husband and Jane Mae needs a daddy. What are you going to do about that? Let's find those boys and you can pick which one you want to marry, how's that for a plan, Carolina?" Ms. Parker queried of her daughter. "Ohhhh, Momma, nooooo, I don't want to marry one of those mean boys! They were horrible to me that day! I could NEVER marry one of them, please no, Momma!" "There you go whining again, now stop that and let's figure out who can marry you then!"

The remainder of the summer was spent working the ranch, taking goodies to the Parker family and the Kammer girls taking turns helping with baby Jane Mae. A few times Izrael could hear his sisters arguing about who was going next. They all talked openly about what a mean and difficult baby she was. None of them seemed to like her. Momma would encourage her girls to be kind and they were kind to the Parker family while they were helping. Momma knew the years ahead would be difficult to maintain a cordial relationship with the Parker family, but she was determined to make it work.

Izrael rarely saw Carolina. When he worked at their house he was outside working and only saw her if she stepped out to hang laundry or sit with the baby on the porch. One August morning while Izrael was trimming bushes out in front of their house, he saw Carolina and Jane Mae on the porch and could not help but be thankful for dodging that bullet; so much so he almost said it out loud! Izrael wrote all these thoughts in his journal. He kept the journal in a safe place, the same place he kept Grandpa K's diary, hidden from anyone else being able to read it. He wondered how Grandpa K would have felt about Izrael reading his diary. Maybe someone would find his one day, a grandson maybe? Would there be any curses to break? The thought was invigorating to Iz, and a little bit unsettling.

CHAPTER 42

"THE UNENDING CHARADE"

Poor Carolina never did find a husband, nor a daddy for baby Jane Mae. She and her mother continued to live in the valley and worked to raise Jane Mae on their own, with help from the very kind Kammer family. There was still one detail everyone had forgotten; everyone but Carolina and Ms. Parker, that is. Carolina had added Izrael Shane Kammer to Jane Mae's birth certificate shortly after she was born. As far as the law was concerned, Jane Mae carried the last name, Kammer, and would always be a Kammer.

"Always a Kammer," Carolina would chant to baby Jane Mae through the years. As Jane Mae began to talk, she chanted the little tune along with her momma. Jane Mae would giggle and chant louder as her momma joined in with her. It became almost a ritual to chant the tune over and over. "Always a Kammer, always a Kammer, always a Kammer, Jane Mae! Always a Kammer, always a Kammer, always a Kammer, Jane Mae!"

The nickname stuck after several years and by the time Jane Mae was 12 years old, she insisted on being called "Kammer-Jane-Mae." Carolina and her momma had chosen to home school Jane Mae to avoid questions about her last name. This was also about the same time that the Kammer family stopped helping the Parker family. When Jane-Mae turned up pregnant before she turned 13 and began accusing boys in the valley of raping her, the Kammer family bowed out. They knew a pattern had stuck, and the curse was continuing, but they would be no part of the continuation.

Over the many years that followed, Kammer-Jane-Mae had several more children, and they now have children. Her oldest grandson, Marcus, is well-known in the mountain valley for being a drug lord. He parks his fancy car at the bottom of the hill, outside of the canyon, and walks up to his grandmother (Kammer-Jane-Mae)'s house. He often stands on the front porch of the mobile home and looks out over the Kammer ranch. He remembers the stories his momma told him, when Grandma Kammer-Jane-Mae was living in a camper. She had snuck her camper deep into the canyon of the property owned by her "father," Izrael Shane Kammer. She was forever determined to somehow live on the Kammer Ranch property.

According to Marcus' momma, the camper was small and dingey, only Grandma Kammer-Jane-Mae was ever in it. No one else could stand the smells or the tiny space. Many times she would see strangers hiking nearby and she always screamed at them to chase them away. She often talked about one couple that had walked by, talking quietly with each other. She opened the camper door and loudly asked who they were. The man stopped, turned right towards her and told her his name and his wife's name. Grandma Kammer-Jane-Mae remembered the wife's name. To herself she had whispered, "Oh, my little sister! I want to run to you and tell you who I am!" But she didn't. Instead, she told the man that she had a gun, and she was not afraid to use it, so they better get away! The couple turned and went back down

"The Unending Charade"

the road, then quickly out of the canyon. Grandma Kammer-Jane-Mae laughed hysterically over this story every time she told it. She thought she had won. She thought she would be the long lost, most loved daughter of the Kammer family. Things did not turn out that way. Once Marcus' momma finally convinced her to leave the camper, she and Grandma Kammer-Jane-Mae began researching and reading stories about the Kammer family and that was when they came across the truth.

Marcus believed the truth only made her more determined and a little crazier. Grandma Kammer-Jane-Mae had bought her mobile home then secretly purchased a small piece of land on the hillside that overlooked the Kammer family home. She always believed one day it would all belong to her.

Since learning the truth of her birth, Kammer-Jane-Mae has remained inside her mobile home, sad that the land can never be hers. She was never a Kammer. She was lied to by her own mother. Life has never been the same. The joy she felt when she first moved onto the hillside, overlooking the family she always wanted to be a part of, was gone forever. Never a Kammer. Just plain Jane-Mae Parker. She would never know who her father was, or could she somehow go back and trace her mother's past? She was not sure she wanted to, as her energy was so very depleted. "Never a Kammer," is all Grandma Jane-Mae said these days, as she sat in her chair by the window that looked out over the land. Her chair creaked on the worn-out floor and almost echoed her words, "Never a Kammer, never a Kammer, never a Kammer-Jane-Mae! Never a Kammer, never a Kammer, never a Kammer-Jane-Mae!"

As Marcus stood on the front porch, looking out over the Kammer family ranch, hearing his grandmother chanting those words, he thought to himself, "Maybe you're not a Kammer,

INTO THE CANYON

Grandma Jane-Mae, but a Parker, and this Parker has plans for our future and all this Kammer land." His eyes stopped when he spotted something shiny on the ground, glimmering against the sunlight.

The woodpecker still pecks, and the land is still loved. The Kammer family ranch lives on, and so does Izrael's poem, in the form of a song.

> "The Cowboy"
>
> *The Cowboy straddles horses and wears a big sombrero,*
> *Shoots it out with outlaws and the Mexican vaquero*
>
> *The tough guy rides the ranges and packs a heavy gun,*
> *Sings to horse and cattle as he rides beneath the sun*
>
> *At night when work is done, he throws a bedroll in the clay,*
> *His pistol in its holster, hopes to make it one more day*
>
> *My Paw-Paw wrote that poem,*
> *about the cowboy from the north*
> *The young man was inspired, back in '44*
>
> *Scribbled on old parchment, by a 2:00 a.m. nightlight*
> *Kerosene oil lantern trains a cowboy's point of sight*
>
> *Oh the cowboy, the cowboy, the cowboy in me....*
> *The Cowboy....*
>
> Words and Music: Victor O. Medina and grandson,
> Christopher J. Baker

ABOUT THE AUTHOR

I have been writing this story since I was a little girl, playing with my sister and brother, on the beautiful ranch our father grew up on and took care of throughout his life. I remember sitting on a big boulder, on the hillside, looking down at the house and property and dreaming of one day sharing it with my future family.

I was born in the closest town (with a hospital) to this ranch and spent just a few months of my life living on the ranch, before my parents moved for an improved livelihood. We never stopped going to the ranch on vacations and the very best of my childhood memories were from those vacations. It became our second home. The memories still echo through the trees and *"Into the Canyon"* of this mountain property.

Most of my life has been living in Albuquerque, New Mexico, where my husband, Vernon, and I live now. We share a love of the mountains and hope to ultimately retire in the northern New Mexico community which inspired this book.

My love of writing is where this book started, many years ago, when it felt mostly like a place to be creative. The fact that it turned into a fiction novel takes my breath away. God's hand is all over it, as I could never have done this without Him leading me, page after page.

FURTHER READING

"Into the Canyon" is the first in a trilogy of the Kammer Family.

CPSIA information can be obtained
at www.ICGtesting.com
Printed in the USA
BVHW042045200223
658864BV00002B/20

9 781662 868511